Doubles

CHRISTOPHER NEVE was born in 1942. He is a painter who has written and taught on art extensively. His *Unquiet Landscape* (Faber) was recommended as a book of the year by both *The Financial Times* and *The Observer*. His novel *Doubles* is a masked anti-biography in which all the characters are fictitious, except for one. The cover incorporates a detail from his oil painting *Glacier* (2009).

To Phillip
from
Christopher Neve .

Doubles

a novel

Christopher Neve

Sur ce teint fauve et brun le fard était superbe.

Baudelaire, *Les Fleurs du Mal*

©Christopher Neve 2015
ISBN 0-936315-39-3

STARHAVEN, 42 Frognal, London NW3 6AG
books@starhaven.org.uk
www.starhaven.org.uk

Typeset in Dante by John Mallinson
Printed by CPI, 38 Ballard's Lane, London N3 2BJ

1

LAST there is the problem of evil.

You remember all this. I write you this letter in the hope that in the end you will obtain forgiveness, and perhaps even peace of mind. As if that were ever possible. *Cher soi-même. Cher fou.* It is appropriate that on the very first page I am, like Don Quixote, shown to be insane. I had intended to mention this in an off-hand way, to slip it in inconspicuously. Narratives of insanity should begin in the middle of a sentence. But starting here, *chère âme perdue,* I write as much for my own sake as for yours. The actions and events I shall describe belong to either or both of us and we are trapped in skins which are not our own. I shall write in French and write quickly. I have a mania for shortness. Well then, dear self, *cher psychopath,* because we both know that equilibrium is among the first obstacles to freedom, and that nothing is real until it is remembered, I begin by speaking of endings. *J'espère que tu sois pardonné.* I follow the scent.

It was September. Everything ending. Summer ending. Menton 1953. Nothing much built yet along the edge of the sea between the town and the hotel. The long yellow curve. Cafés with chairs on the tables, and awnings folded up because of the coming wind. On my way back to the hotel I was oppressed by the sense of endings. Aged 12, I wondered fervently if I could keep faith with the person I next intended to be.

The only thing which seemed never to end was the sound of blasting that had kept up all summer. It came from the mountainside where they were building a new road. The sound, a double crump, rolled slowly along above the bay as if you should be able to see it.

I had left the monkey on the beach, a monkey with a strap around its waist. It sat scratching itself on beach tables or looking miserably out to sea as though there was nothing worth looking at in the town. It belonged to the man who hired out deckchairs. For a week I had hung about, trying to draw it. It had no biography, but evidently it held plenty against me. Its antics made me laugh. Meeting it was like meeting a low-spirited version of myself whom I had unpardonably wronged somehow. The self or the other? For fifteen minutes at a time it sat worrying.

It was a kilometre back to the hotel. I crossed the scorching road by the garage with its light blue morning glory, smells of oil and vulcanizing and the sounds of spanners being dropped in the gloom. There was a shortcut past a bust of Marshal Foch commanding rows of canna in a municipal garden. An iron cockerel which never stopped crowing. As I began to walk along the top of the low wall by the sea, I noticed that Mr. Marakat, who always monopolized the bathing-raft, was in position as usual. He was burned almost black by this time of year and repelled boarders effortlessly by cursing. I could tell that he was watching me. Inland there were yellow villas, their stucco pitted with the eczema of small-arms fire, and behind them a narrow tract of land used for vegetable gardens, and beyond that, running parallel to the road towards the border, was the railway from Nice to Ventimiglia and San Remo.

That hotel. A place of loss and cocktails. I see it now as tragic and menacing, in E minor, a place with a relentless end, where something was going to happen from which there was no escape and there was no option but for me to remain there and endure it. At the time, it stood in the bright light, far enough away without being too far, almost too delicate to examine. Its old-time air was faint, its simple but not inelegant rectangle, pre-1910 but unadorned, slightly taller than it was long, faded like a book left out in the sun. Greenish shutters. A row of palm trees in front. A visitable past, self-effacing, unobtrusive, hardly worth noticing.

I stayed here with my father for at least two months each summer and had done so since I was eight. That nothing ever happened in the hotel except for this one incident was of its essence. Unhappeningness, even seen unblurred by backward vision, was about as close to its air of the past as it was possible to get, and inescapable. There was an eau-de-Nil letter-writing room in it with a roll-top desk. Both physically and psychologically the building was at a safe distance from Menton, or sometimes Mentone, place of invalids and carnivals, and at a safe distance from the border – in fact, only a few hundred metres – so that it was both Italian and French. Its delicate identities overlapped.

The same cast had grown old here year after year. Some of the women had bent double. They looked at the sea sideways. As I approached I saw that my father's shutters were closed against the heat. He would be working. Mrs Suarez was on her balcony. She liked to say of herself that she had a sense of humour, but never showed the slightest sign of one. The erect, carrot-coloured hair, terrified expression and powdered cleavage of poor, pregnant Miss Quail, were visible at her window in the roof. Mrs Arvold Cole, who wrote books about her English garden, was sitting at a table by the main door. *'Il faut cultiver son jardin'*, she said all the time. There was Henze, like a concierge, whom I suspected of learning everything there was to know about the other residents because he never spoke but only secretly observed, and the insomniac Monsieur Lefèbvre who did nothing but complain. He never failed to remark, 'Twenty years ago this fish would have been properly cooked,' or 'Twenty years ago, when people said they would do something, they did it.' On the terrace was the moustached man whom I had found naked in a corridor one evening, unable to remember his room number.

The hotel lift was operated by a *blessé* called Mossman, whose job it was to open and close the door and drag luggage about. In fact, he mostly avoided luggage because it was as much as he could do to drag his game leg about, his heavy boot being luggage enough. Instead, he bowed and scraped, touched his forelock in an unctuous way and paid compliments. When he opened the lift door to people he practically drowned them in compliments. He used every known compliment and more soap and oil than anyone would think possible, smiling all the time. He did not just get on my father's nerves, he drove him to distraction. My father always referred to him as 'That half-wit Mossman'.

Madame Olga Alba was emerging from the lift and detaching herself from Mossman as I went across the hall. There were whitish gladioli in a fan-shaped vase, demurely elegant, outmoded. Muffled light struck gently off mirrors. Madame Alba, who often expressed her opinion that moths are the ghosts of butterflies, knew about rubato. She paused for a moment for effect, nodded at me and said '*La brume estompe les lointains*'. Each year she contrived to involve herself with every man in the hotel. She never kept them more than a week or two.

All this was predictable and seemed to have been going on forever. Upstairs, my father would be sure to say, looking me up and down, 'Oh Lord. You're not c-coming into lunch like that, are you?'

He would be in low spirits. He always was. Most of the time he spent in his room because, if he did not go out, he could be sure not to meet anyone he knew. I believed he had marked paranoiac tendencies.

At lunch, pushing the melon about on his plate as though it annoyed him – he was permanently angry – he would tick me off for drawing. He was very much against unnecessary drawing. In fact, he despised all the arts and went to great lengths to avoid them.

'Have you been doing anything unusual?'
'There was a monkey on the beach.'
'A what?'
'A monkey. I was drawing it.'
'A b-bad habit.'
'Drawing?'
'It gets you nowhere. You will find that it isn't remotely of use in the wider world. Well, you know what *I* think.'

And then we would sit silent. He would crack his fingers between courses. Groups of cyclists, in caps with the peaks turned up, would pass beneath the window, adolescents on their way to buy comics and pornography over the border. Also the unemployed, with fishing rods.

But, in the event, it turned out that this was not what either of us said. When everyone was seated in the dining-room, including the small man thought to be related to ex-King Zog of Albania, and Pascal, the waiter, had begun to go slowly about with a tray on his shoulder, the day abruptly changed. Outside, the sea became dark. Banana leaves began to thrash the windows. Torrential rain. Rain to flatten the salvias, knock blooms off bougainvilleas and make dust hop on garden paths. Rain to make cars hiss, and a crocodile of seminarians, holding their hats on, run for cover. Rain, the first for weeks, to drown out conversation and keep up furiously all afternoon. Rain to wash the summer away and finally put an end to the blue of the sea.

And rain to wash away part of the mountainside above the hotel, where the blasting had been going on, and send a cascade of mud and rocks with a roar down on to the railway line – halting in its tracks the afternoon train, the luxury train from Nice, on its dash behind the houses towards Italy and points south.

My father was in his room, reading Scherau's *Cent Pensées de la Nuit*, a favourite book of his. When the rain stopped I went up to look at the landslide. Some stragglers, pushing their bicycles, out of curiosity did the same. A frustrated locomotive of colossal size, emitting steam from every orifice, was waiting in an olive grove. Smoke hung in the branches of the trees and in telephone wires. An enormous cloud of smoke arced over the small building up the track, partly obscuring it, to which the driver had gone to report the difficulty by phone. Two very old people, a man and a woman, the man with a stick, walked slowly towards the engine on a path beside the rails and barely glanced at it.

The fireman climbed down from the cab and had a shouted conversation with the driver about water. The locomotive could not wait there long with steam up and no water. There was a disagreement. Eventually the fireman, carrying a metal tool with which to lift manhole covers, set off in the direction of the town. Fifty metres up the line was the pile of mud and rocks. In the coaches I could see outlandish-looking people, gilt table-lamps, lavish curtains. Some of the passengers distorted their features by pressing them against carriage windows and looked as though they came from an unknown race. Others had partly opened windows and dangled their arms out of them as if caught in lobster pots. Insects made the post-rain noise of cine-projectors. Over the noise of steam a nightingale may have sung. In this way the world stuck.

2

And then came free.

'Is that you?' a voice said, and I saw a woman looking at me, laughing. She may have been 30. Black, vivacious, smart. Very red lipstick. Shirt roughly the colour of the lavender at Grasse. Such glamour did not un-nerve me. She had opened a carriage door.

'Pencils for Matabeleland,' she said, and handed me down the following: an oyster-white suitcase, a circular red hatbox, a leopard-skin coat and a picture wrapped in brown paper. Then she handed me down herself. Long legs. After which she asked, looking down the slope, 'Isn't that a hotel?' and we set off towards it with me carrying her luggage.

When I glanced round I saw that we were at the head of a procession, many other passengers having followed suit. Oh well, I thought, the hotel at the moment is only half full. It will give Signora Pizzechemi and Pascal something to do. Lipstick took back her coat and put her arm through mine. In my mind I had already come up with my childhood name for her, Lipstick Matabele. I never knew her real name.

'It's not much of a hotel,' I said, betraying it effortlessly, 'but I come here every year.' How else do you practice insouciance at 12?

'You're not interested in psychiatry, are you?' she said, as we came to the hotel. 'I went to Sigmund Freud's house in London once. I waited a long time on the doorstep in the rain with a German woman. When I went in I found that his desk, bookshelves, every available surface, was covered with tomb figures, small ancient figures from Greece, Rome and Egypt. Freud didn't like art but he had collected these figures. He handled them all the time. He was dying of cancer of the jaw. The reason he liked the figures was that they had survived by being buried. As in the unconscious,' she added, helpfully.

Then she looked at the hotel and said 'Youpi!' and we went in. Hard marble floor. High heels.

Signora Pizzechemi came out of her cluttered office behind the reception desk. I knew to my cost that she had a prickly face. She was the widow of Signore Pizzechemi who died when I was ten, so the hotel was now hers. Both she and her husband had come from the toe of Italy. Neither of them much liked guests. She allocated Lipstick Matabele a room and turned to unhook the key from the rack.

'It's not much of a room,' I said disloyally. 'It's on the top floor at the back.'

Signora Pizzechemi disregarded my remark and her eyes widened as the rest of the train people crowded into her genteel foyer. A group of them, delirious with poker, immediately turned the furniture round and continued playing.

Lipstick said, 'Don't think twice. It's the room I would have chosen. That man in pyjamas has been dealt miracle hand after miracle hand.' Mossman, hopping about in a fever of excitement, fawningly opened the lattice door of the lift for her, and while the cage hesitated she whispered in my ear, 'Three of clubs. If he doesn't catch one on the turn his chances of making a flush have reduced to nine to one.'

Before the lift moved upwards I saw Signora Pizzechemi's eyes narrow again, and then really narrow, as one of the arrivals, taking drumsticks from the back of his neck, beat out a drum solo on the desk-bell and hotel register. To her amazement she saw that behind him waited a cardinal, in red skull cap, and a trio of animated-looking middle-aged women with black net on large white Italian hats and stylish Roman clothes cut on the bias.

The presence of the cardinal prompted some problems of

precedence and a good deal of hand-kissing, which he put up with condescendingly and with a hint of mockery. 'Eminence,' Signora Pizzechemi whispered.

'I'd rather not talk about it,' said a heavy man with a brown face, an English accent and impressively full beard. He also was in the queue. 'I'm the only person in this room who might actually make some money while he's here.' Then the lift with us in it went through the pretty Italianate ceiling and the scene was lost to view.

Behaving like a bell-hop I showed Lipstick Matabele to her room, spread out her luggage and unhitched the shutters to reveal not much of a view into the top of a palm tree with the hotel yard below it. By the back door to the kitchen Monsieur Carrafancq's Alsatian lay on its side, trying to get some sleep despite the flies. When Lipstick came and stood beside me, looking down at the same view, I felt an unfamiliar pang of intimacy (not having a mother) and my imagination raced to come up with ways of describing her irresistible smell. A chord with three sharps in it? Hay? Some word in botany or philosophy I did not yet know? Something deep-rooted to do with coming home?

Already we could hear the clanging of picks and shovels which meant that men had begun clearing the line soon to take her away from me. In my imagination I may even have sighed.

Still looking at the lack of view, she said, as if to herself, 'I am mostly alone but in great profusion. Who needs always to be looking at the sea? I like the view from the backs of buildings better than the front, don't you?'

It had not occurred to me but I said yes. When we left the window she unwrapped her picture and propped it up. 'To do with the secret life of objects,' she explained. 'The sadness within the corners of a box, that sort of thing. See what you think.'

It was an uphill task to think anything. A small, reticent, cardboard-coloured oil painting showing a few objects huddled together on a shelf. They included a funnel of the sort used in garages for pouring oil. Some of the utensils partly masked others as people often do in group photographs. About my main interest in life being pictures, I opened my mouth to make some comment, but Lipstick immediately hushed me and we continued together to evaluate the qualities of the painting in silence for several minutes. 'Don't,' she said eventually.

'Don't what?'

'Don't interrupt a picture.'

'Don't interrupt a picture?'

'Yes. And don't think you can discuss it afterwards either, except perhaps in terms of something else.'

'What sort of something else?'

'Well, you could discuss this one in terms of, for instance, jazz or table-tennis. Silence is better. I suppose, if you feel you must, you could say that it's the colour of bone, soap, straw, paper, pottery, factories, dust. The colour of Bologna Minor.'

'It gets you no further?'

'Hardly. Are you repressed?'

'No.'

'Living here among the old people.'

I did not think she had yet had time to observe the old people.

'What you need is much less quietness. Quietness isn't necessarily a sign of good character, you know. Try to abandon the happy medium.'

She seized me suddenly by the wrist and hauled me out of the door. After we had clattered down the service stairs she ran through the kitchens and out into the yard where Monsieur Carrafancq's Alsatian got up, causing a commotion at the end of its tether, and Pascal's derelict-looking motorbike stood by the wall.

'Hurry up. Get on,' she shouted, already heaving it off its stand and beginning to kick the starter. I heard the black-market petrol slosh in the tank. His motorbike was Pascal's only un-pawned possession and he rode it sedately. It was heavy, Italian, ex-army, sand-coloured, with white numbers painted on it. The engine fired. There was a deafening riot of exhaust against the back of the building. I jumped on, put my arms round Lipstick's negligible waist and she let out the yelping clutch. We shot round the side of the hotel onto the coast road, and the sea began to go past in an exaggerated manner until in no time we were at the frontier.

Before our arrival, it must have been peaceful at the border control. Two limp flags. A couple of striped barriers. A parked bus with its engine running. A diminutive Fiat Topolino. One gendarme asleep on his feet like a mule, another listlessly examining a passport. He spent a long time flicking through the pages, turning it round in his hands to peer at the photograph, then bent way down to look in at the driver of the Topolino. All this as we approached. Lipstick Matabele changed down several times, waved at the gendarmes and, gunning her engine, steered between them. Their belts and holsters looked worn out, tired by the long afternoon. She made a wide turn and accelerated fiercely back the way we had come. She had momentarily alleviated their boredom and the gendarmes watched her exit with regret. We narrowly missed the adolescent cyclists on their return journey, the pornography safely in their saddle-bags with their tyre-repair kits, and were back at the hotel almost before we had gone.

But it was no longer the same hotel. During the short time that we had been absent, it and its previous cast had been extensively altered. My gentle friend Pascal was barely recognizable. His normally shadowed eyes were blazing. Sardonic smile and sallow, hollow cheeks were gone, replaced by a look of scarlet panic. Signora Pizzechemi had dashed to the kitchen and punched Monsieur Carrafancq, knocking him to the floor as he made béarnaise sauce. And poor Miss Quail, in the absence of anyone to help her, had set off to drive herself to the maternity hospital, her Airedale with its head out of the car window. Every time she had a contraction Miss Quail howled and the Airedale howled in sympathy. This information from Madame Alba, the only person apart from me among the hotel guests who had defected to the train people.

We sat in the narrow strip of garden by the sea. The new

arrivals drank cocktails: Waldorfs, White Ladies, Sidecars, Raffles Knockouts, Manhattans. 'And don't forget the dash of fresh lemon with a cherry and salt,' someone called to Pascal.

Inside the hotel the permanent residents made their way to the dining-room and arranged themselves at their tables in the lamplight, not talking, as though in a lit-up display cabinet. They were joined by Monsieur Chaise-Dieu and his family, always late. Monsieur Chaise-Dieu, despised by Signora Pizzechemi, lived in the hotel annex in a state of chaos. He permitted no cleaning. His wife, a small viperish woman, was completely indistinguishable from his sister. He himself was humorous, bearlike, slow, and always elevating trivial incidents into great occasions. Upstairs lived his father, of immense age, who had recently remarried.

Lipstick Matabele regarded all these people with interest. Then she looked at the small black book in which I had made drawings of them. She sat with it on her knee and gave each drawing the same prolonged, silent attention to which she had subjected the painting in her room. She did not look up. A Vespa went by. The wake from a boat which had passed a long time ago worked itself out among the rocks beneath the jetty. From the far side of the bay, where the old town was, came the just audible squeal of a bugle band and the distant sound of crowds. There was the blip of a firework. A rocket went up and, disintegrating at a height without a puttering noise, allowed its fragments to drift leisurely down on their reflections. Some saint's day or other. The cardinal would know which one.

Lipstick Matabele looked through my drawing-book a second time, glanced across at my father and the others in the dining-room and said 'Youpi!' more than once.

'Could you recognize them?' I asked.

'Yes, but the drawings are more than likenesses, I think. You have drawn the people but in the process you have also drawn a little world of suffering, catastrophes and predicaments.'

'I meant just to draw portraits.'

'You didn't recognize that the flesh has its own earnestness?'

'How?'

'In drawing old people you remind me that we live solemnly and behave busily without glancing at our…'

'Our what?'

'I was going to say at our vulnerability.'

'But that's not it?'

'Not exactly. More complicated than that. Karl Barth says something like, "Terribly thin are the threads of knowing not-knowing which is here presented to us." That's what is in your drawings.'

Behind me the cardinal remarked, 'Exegesis or hermeneutics?'

'I am deaf,' said the man with the brown face and a beard like a swarm of bees, 'but at least I know my handicap. Do you know yours?'

When Lipstick suggested we put our tables together in a long line in the garden and have dinner, she and I went to the kitchen to see what we could find.

No doubt there was always a degree of pandemonium in the kitchen at meal times – heat, hurry, cursing, noise – but the skill of waiters when emerging into the dining-room is to appear calm, unhurried, discreet, stylish. All this was now lost.

Monsieur Carrafancq, who came from a family of heroic Pyrenean mountain guides, was completely helpless, sobbing on a box, and a sous-chef called Didier had taken over. He was slapping monkfish about. A second waiter had also been brought in at short notice to help Pascal, but he was elderly, had spent the war in hiding and was still inclined to hide, so was not of much use. Homard à la Parisienne, selle de chevreuil sauce grand veneur, savarin aux fruits à la liqueur de Maraschino, bottles of champagne and Château Robine we carried outside. In the dining-room we could see Pascal set a monkfish down in front of Madame Chaise-Dieu or her sister-in-law. She was yellow with nicotine or jaundice. The fish, also yellow, seemed to stare balefully back at her. She and it were alike, their expressions of mutual distaste identical. Both had suffered life-long from prejudice against their appearance.

'Man cannot endure a meaningless life,' the cardinal said, gratefully spreading his napkin, tucking it in.

'More than the world,' said the deaf man. 'Did I hear the word dinner?'

I sat next to Lipstick Matabele and thought contentedly about the little world of suffering, catastrophe and predicaments while attempting to draw the cardinal in my book under the table, surreptitiously and with difficulty. He was dark-skinned, old, short-sighted, and wore small, round wire-framed glasses like a devil.

'Hell,' I whispered to Lipstick. 'I can't see and there's no time.'

'Give someone endless time and plenty of clean paper,' she said, 'and they'll produce next to nothing. Give them no time and the back of an envelope and they'll produce something wonderful.'

Lights were switched on in the American warship moored outside the harbour.

The cardinal had an ironic expression. The wine was obviously not what he was used to.

'He thinks he is the cat's whiskers,' Lipstick Matabele said. 'You must put that in too. Where there are cardinals there is always a good cellar.'

'Every woman is at least twenty women,' someone said.

'Not all at the same time.'

'Yes, all at the same time.'

'Saint Francis Xavier, in the church of Bom Jesus at Goa.'

'And you? How many are you?' asked someone else of an American woman who was evidently interested in hair products.

'Including your alter ego.'

'Well, God is three.'

The cardinal spoke with his eyes tight shut as though asleep. 'Isn't it worth at least considering that the God you don't believe in is one that doesn't exist?'

'Mary Magdalene then.'

'A fish the colour of a relic.'

'Why her?'
'Several women in one. The woman taken in adultery, the third woman at the foot of the cross, the washer of feet. All the same person.'
'In fact, not herself at all.'
'Certainly herself, but as several different women.'
'If I eat this, I may be ill for a month or probably for the rest of my life.'
'You mean, one of you may.'
'Every one is the other.'
'The psychic other?'
'Of course. And full of contradictions.'
'Schopenhauer's poodle was called – '
'Hermeneutics or exegesis?' the cardinal said. Zoot, I thought. The train people are not ones for trivia or gossip.

Lipstick took my hand, laughing. 'He looks similar to Edward Lear, that man with a beard like a swarm. You don't remember Edward Lear?'

I said I did, but I was lying.

'He lived very close to here when he was old. At San Remo, just over the frontier. He hated his nose. Although he didn't like San Remo he built a small villa there, with only the railway between it and the sea. He and his cat had only lived there a short time when a hotel sprang up in front of it, completely blocking the view. A blank back wall, blinding white, was all he could see. So, using the last of his money, he built a second villa slightly further along with an unimpeded view. He took great trouble to ensure that the arrangement of rooms in the new villa was the same as in the first one so that Foss, his beloved cat, who was 16 years old and blind, would not bump into things and bang his head. The day they moved in, Foss died. He is buried under a rose-bush on the terrace. If you go there you can see the grave. Trains rush between it and the sea.'

Listening to this, I noticed that Mr. Marakat, he of the bathing-raft, had sat down with the train people at the other end of the table and was watching me closely.

Someone was trying to attract my attention.

'Come, you. Come and stand by me,' said a cadaverous-looking man with a thin reddish beard and greenish-pink skin, beckoning me energetically and pointing at a place on the ground next to his chair. When I arrived there I found him to be Dutch, cheesy and pitted in close-up, with a breath of milk and chives. Grasping me by the scruff of the neck, he whispered, 'You like tricks? Tricks? Oblige me. Simple. I pinch your neck and you move your mouth as if speaking. No voice. Remain silent. I squeeze. Move your lips only.'

Terrified, I kept my eyes on Lipstick Matabele and she smiled at me encouragingly, with radiance, from the other side of the table. Her radiance would have made anyone's terror unquestionably worthwhile.

Everyone was quiet and paid attention to me and the greenish Dutchman.

'What is your name?' he asked me in French.

Pinch. 'Voltaire. What's yours?' He gave me a woman's voice.

'Stop that,' he said, much taken aback by my insolence. 'My name is van der Beek.'

Pinch. 'Are you sure?'

'Certainly I am sure. They gave me that name and drew on my head in icy water.'

Pinch. 'You were there?'

'Why do you think I'm not who I say I am?'

Pinch. 'Because you're divided between you and me. That's obvious to everyone. *Olleke Bolleke, Bebusolleke, Olleke Bolleke, Knoll.*'

'I won't have this.'

Pinch. 'Put an end to it then. If you are silent, I am silent.'

He thought for a moment, then asked dejectedly, 'So who in the world am I?'

Pinch. 'Certain kinds of absence.'

'Absence?'

Pinch. 'Yes, absence and contradiction. Darkness, solitude, silence. Things reason can't dispel.'

He feigned extravagant despair. It was easy to imagine tears coursing down his green cheeks. Then suddenly he laughed uproariously, stood up, put a kind arm round my shoulders. Applause. We bowed. Whatever it was, with my help he had got it off his chest rather quickly.

'What happened?' I asked Lipstick when she welcomed me back.

'You were clever and spoke about things you know nothing about.' Ever since, when declaiming on topics I know nothing about, I have felt the cruel pinch of the Dutch ventriloquist's fingers on the nape of my neck.

But now everyone was looking with agitated attention at the dining-room as if at a traffic accident. Pascal, driven frantic by the new waiter's slowness and ineptitude, had become entangled with him. Their trays locked. Two monkfish were dropped from a height. A gold tooth flashed as Pascal took hold of the elderly waiter's arm and bit his hand with hatred, sinking in his incisors with all the pent-up ferocity of a summer spent being condescended to and ordered about morning, noon and night by people he could not stand the sight of and who should have been waiting on *him*.

Before anyone realised what was happening, Lipstick Matabele had run into the hotel, helped the grappling waiters off the floor and led them gently back to where we sat in the garden.

'*Un coup de bec.* Nothing more,' remarked the cardinal.

Chairs were found for them, their wounds bound up in napkins by the stylish Italian women. Drinks, food and consolation proffered on all sides. Pascal had once been a choirboy at Rouen. A sad-faced treble he must have made in carved stalls. Now he was so unused to sympathy that he burst into tears. The second waiter, Emilio, sat nursing his bite. Shown tenderness, he said, 'Bastà. Just appetite.' And we all sat watching Signora Pizzechemi at work alone until my father and the other residents left in disgust for an early night, and the lit-up fish tank of the dining-room was empty.

In the garden there followed a conversation about Eric Satie, Four Flabby Preludes for a Dog and the Pear-shaped piano pieces. To everyone's delight, Pascal turned out to be an expert on Eckhart. He and the cardinal had a lively discussion about freedom from desire.

But Lipstick Matabele spoke only to me. She looked me in the eyes and spoke to me as follows:

'Listening to music, you listen to yourself. If they weren't obsessive, artists would never get their work done. Language is unstable. Speak of one thing in terms of another. Must all answers take the form of another question?'

Then we talked for a long time about painting.

She caught the eye of the deaf man and smiled. He was sitting far away at the other end of the table. Her red lips pouted and stretched beautifully as she enunciated 'Gauloises Disque Bleu?' Laughing, he produced a blue packet of cigarettes and signalled for it to be passed along to her.

'The deaf are exceptional because they hear with their eyes,' she said to me. 'Did you know that they carry their own language in an imaginary box in front of them? A small theatre of mime to which their faces are the backdrop. In front of their expressions they sign with their hands.'

'But that's not language.'

'It has its own grammar and syntax.'

'You mean it spells out words?'

'No. The deaf don't sign the word for table. They sign the object itself. Shakespeare makes Pyramus say, "I see a voice." Expert lip-readers can read over long distances.'

'Across a room?'

'Yes.'

'Across a road?'

'Yes. So be careful what you say.'

Turning to the deaf man, she remarked quietly, 'We have been talking about pictures.' And he immediately signed back as follows: 'I know. I used to be in silent pictures once.'

Finally the train people with odd-shaped luggage produced their musical instruments. They began to tune them, egged on by Madame Alba. I did not want Lipstick to stop talking. I did not want her to stop talking ever. Not one thing she said have I forgotten. She was the first person who ever spoke to me as if I was an adult. I only understood the occasional phrase, but I can transcribe the rest now without hesitation, like remembering music. 'Much art is based on a theme and variations, with the theme removed.' 'All cats are grey at night.' 'Music begins where language stops.' 'Always remember that you are unique, just like everybody else.' 'There is always the sea.' She said this looking at the horizon. When she said it, she seemed both sad and happy at the same time, as though contemplating some enormous tragedy which nevertheless gave her satisfaction. 'What am I looking for?'

And, long after the stars had come out, the music started and a most surprising thing happened. Madame Olga Alba sang.

She had a terrible voice. But there was something inexplicable about her. She was old but girlish. I had once seen her in pyjamas with little animals on them. Sometimes, but not always, she affected a lisp. Every few weeks she suffered a relapse and was pushed about in a wheelchair, but even as an invalid she exerted a physical attraction. Contradictory, she was both primrose and bullock. Now her hair was in bunches and she had put on a tutu.

'Not E flat,' groaned the guitarist.

She began singing and everything stopped. The syncopated croaking of frogs in the hotel cistern stopped. The eccentrics, intellectuals, glamorous women stopped. Lipstick Matabele stopped. Planets stopped. Loss, longing, despair, all stopped while her cracked cadences played havoc with sad laughter, and there was not a soul hearing her who failed to understand, in the blackness of attempted high notes, that a broken cry contains the mysterious essence of all pain and the meaning of life and death.

Next day I was woken by the sound of the locomotive. Very early in the morning all those people must have walked up the path to the train. Now the carriages were trampling the line, gathering speed.

I found that Lipstick Matabele had written in the back of my sketchbook, in bright red lipstick, *Nous restons sur notre soif.* She had enormous writing.

My evening with the people off the train had infuriated my father and we left the next day. I protested at leaving so suddenly but he said that it was good for children to learn disappointment.

The following winter the hotel was torn down despite its pretty Italianate ceilings, the victim of a road-widening scheme. When he told me about it, my father remarked that it had been 'n-no more than *assez confortable*.'

No doubt you of all people will remember that when I hurried to the beach to see the monkey it had already gone. And that the kiss I received on each cheek from Signora Pizzechemi was like a wasp sting. And that when I said good-bye to Pascal for the last time he smiled sadly, limply shook my hand, and said 'Hello', as though he understood perfectly well that only now was he beginning his long journey in my memory.

3

In Paris I always kept an eye open for my mother. My father told me that she had died when I was two, but I did not believe him.

'How did she die?' I asked. For years he would not reply.

My motherless adolescence in Paris was passed like an illness, as if I had a high temperature. It came to the period of the Algerian war, Existentialism, the French Left and Juliette Gréco. I did not know myself. The boy I had been at Menton was dead. But always at the back of my mind was the idea that we constantly cross and recross each other's paths, and that the people off the Menton train were here if I could but recognize them. Once I thought I saw the woman with the yellow face at Salle Gaveau. One hot summer when the Metro stopped in the catacomb and I hung there on the strap with the rest of the living dead, I was almost certain that I peered into the face of the deaf man in the wide hat. They say it is the first 12 years of his life that form a man's imagination, and for most of those years I had spent my summers at Menton. I could never accept that Lipstick Matabele had been only temporary.

Then, when I was 19, I saw an etching. It was in the window of a run-down, yellow-fronted gallery in the rue St. Louis-en-L'Île. In those days the shops in the rue St. Louis-en-L'Île seemed always to be full of red and green parrot tulips. The print was in sepia, the ink of the cuttlefish. The subject of the etching was a drowning. That is, it was an architectural subject which, in the middle distance, showed the body of a drowned woman pulled from the Seine, lying in a pool of water on the pavé of Quai Montebello, her head tilted up, her jaw in the air. A row of badauds, on-lookers, was perched on the wall, and there were faces at the windows of the Hôtel des Trois Balances above them. Coils of smoke festooned the tall roofs and attics of the houses, the house-fronts unchanged today although the etching had been done in the 1850s. In the foreground there were iron rings and moored laundry barges.

A gendarme in a cocked hat was directing men to lift the body and carry it to the nearby morgue. The figures were small, an ant-like human melodrama put in to give an architectural subject interest. The woman's bereft child was standing beside her.

'My mother drowned, didn't she?' I said to my father that evening, among his heavy furniture in the Huitième, behind the Madeleine.

'How did you know?'
'I think I remember it.'
'You could not p-possibly remember it.'
'I was there, wasn't I?'
'You were there but you certainly did not see her drown.'
'Where did this happen? Was it in Paris?'
'No.'
'Why won't you tell me?'
'Christ, if you must know, it happened at B-Biarritz. There

are some things which are much better not discussed. It would only do harm.'

'Why?' But he would not talk about it.

From that moment I knew that I was the product of a catastrophe which I could not remember. I had witnessed something terrible before I even had a memory. Death by water.

4

When I got off the boat, I saw a small character in a tallish hat, with hanging-down black hair, who seemed to be watching me.

(This incident in Venice was like a paragraph in brackets.)

Dear God, I thought. They never told me it would be the *acqua alta*. From now on I was to be troubled by sullen water which lay along the horizon of my imagination like an incoming tide. The fondamenti were under water and shallow waves were sucking at the steps of the Gesuati. I hauled my suitcase, full of equipment with which I would make the wax mould, to the nearest pensione. I liked the room they gave me. In it was a blackened mirror and an outsize escritoire. When I opened the shutters I saw a narrow canal like a drain with a funeral gondola wedged in it between high walls. Tarnished gilding. Words went through my head: rancour, grudge, succubus, incubus. I was here to make a life-mask of the painter Georges Idris.

Next morning I went to the Pensione Seguso, on the Zattere. The character in the tall hat was in the hall. Uncertain whether it was the right place, I went in twice. He was still squatting there, like a numbered stage instruction. Each time I went in he stood up and then sat down again as I went out. Had I not come in, would he still have stood up and sat down? He seemed a feature of my unconscious.

I spoke to him. Instead of replying he looked away from me into his own middle-distance. He exhibited profound indifference to what I had to say and did not reply.

I asked to see Idris. The receptionist told me that he lived here but had already gone out.

'This is Nils,' she said, indicating the up-and-down character in the tall hat. 'He is the assistant of Georges Idris. Nils, do you know where Georges Idris has gone?'

Both the receptionist and I looked hopefully at Nils, who eventually said, 'Had it been possible.'

'I believe Georges Idris usually goes to the Accademia first thing,' the receptionist said. 'He is expecting you.'

'He knows I'm coming?'

'Certainly.'

We both turned to Nils again for confirmation, but with a minimum of effort he continued to look away. Next time, I thought, I will try addressing him in rhyming couplets. As hats went, it was a terrible hat: grey, with a high crown and black ribbon, evidently brand new. His dyed black hair hung down as though attached to its rim. He had a sharp profile, Expressionist eyes, white skin and abnormally wide, thin lips, above which lay, like a sleeping caterpillar, a long, sparse, soft-whiskered attempt at a moustache.

It was no hardship to walk through the Accademia. The pictures were so good I almost forgot what I had come for. No one answered to the description of Georges Idris until I came to the last room, where Titian's *Pietà* is on display. Idris was undoubtedly the old man seated in front of it and paying it a great deal of attention, so much, in fact, that I did not like to interrupt him. It did not occur to me there might be something the matter with me when I entered and re-entered the room twice, and then three times. Each time the experience was different.

First time. About 10.36 a.m. There sits a rather large and dis-ordered-looking man in his 80s, in a state of excitement, his eyes moving across the Titian as if checking each part in relation to all the others. He hauls himself up and scrutinises a passage of painting at short range.

Second time. What a curious circumstance! I have come to bury this old head in wax, with straws in the nostrils, long enough to make a cast of it. An odd form of intimacy with someone I have never met before. The head is less than ideal.

Flabby, undistinguished, no precision. Double bag under each eye. Chops. A goitre almost. Something of the Balzac toad in a sack. How much better a cat with a Hitler moustache.

Third time. The Titian is dark and seems to fill the whole room. Apart from Idris, no one else here. I walk up and stand beside him wondering if now is the moment when I should introduce myself. I am self-aware. I need not have worried. Before I can say anything, he speaks to me. This occurred just before 11 o'clock. It was a Tuesday.

'But is it finished?' he asked vehemently. 'Titian's late style. That old problem. Since twenty years before he died, everyone thought his late work unfinished. Doubt pleases me no less than knowledge. How much of life remains to old men! I would rather be seen as crazy or incompetent, if my defects please or delude me, than be wise and snarl. Baudelaire said he was both young and very old. Crazed with purpose. I shall miss, above all, the sky. Like great philosophers, Titian takes pains not to be quotable. His most serious ideas are produced not by direct statements but through implication, allusion, repetition, contrast, symbol, irony, context. The astonished dreamer, he is amazed by his unconscious visions. The hardest part is the simple step from inaction to action.'

I had a feeling that he was speaking to me in experimental French, in language that might at any moment give way.

'Oh,' he went on, 'you can resort to artificial paradises, to drunkenness, drugs, prostitutes, occultism, eroticism, dandyism, surrealism, orientalism. You can escape into fantasy, vivid enclosed worlds, well away from reality.'

I seized my chance. 'Well, *I* think,' I said, 'that Titian's late work is certainly finished. Yes, and that he died still trying.'

Idris got up, not without difficulty, and put his arms around me. 'The boy's a genius!' he said. 'I'm so glad you've at last arrived. That little bastard Nils said you wouldn't be here till next week.'

He was inordinately cheerful. I saw at once that he was deformed, deformed in the sense that his appearance bore no relation whatever to his character. He looked lugubrious. In fact, he was sprightly, exuberant and far from taking himself too seriously.

'To Montin's at once,' he said. 'It's not too early for lunch. Life is full of surprises and more bounteous now than it has ever seemed before. I have a great deal to tell you if you'd like to hear it. I have finally become sane. It is the superabundance of old age. I can't wait to tell you what's on my mind. It's a matter of some urgency. You had a good journey? You have somewhere to stay? The acqua alta is an inconvenience, of course. It's why the poor devils live on the piano nobile if they can.'

We went on our way, Venice coming to pieces all around us, and arrived at Montin's. Outside were the prows of tethered gondolas by the Fondamenta di Borgo. Inside were the paintings exchanged forty years before by amateurs in need of a cheap meal. We sat in the big old room in semi-darkness. A man reading alone knocked over his drink, mopped it up with a cloth and wrung the cloth out into his glass so as not to waste any. There is so much interest, and so much comment on life, in this pointless story.

'The matter with Nils,' Idris said apologetically, 'is that, when he was a baby, his mother used to take him with her when she went to visit her boyfriend in prison. It started then, I am certain of it. He played with bricks while waiting for her to finish her conversation through the grille.'

I was excited now to listen to Georges Idris's conversation – I was at this time 20 years old, and the insights of an old artist were worth attention. Here was a man to whom the only passionate life was the life of pictures. Unlike my father, who thought art no more than an attempt to draw attention to oneself, Georges Idris felt fervently that it was the only thing that really mattered. Always in search of an improvement on my father, I was drawn to him, agog. But at first it was hard to take in what he was saying. Not only was his French strangely idiomatic, he was overexcited and needed to calm down. He plied me with unfamiliar delicacies, Venetian specialties, to eat and drink. And the obtrusive conversation of the people at neighbouring tables did not help. A woman was saying, 'The birth took eleven hours, and the whole time the midwife talked of nothing but elephants.' Another said, 'Of course, with chicken stock you need to boil it to kill the microbes.' In the locanda doorway a cat, unaccountably and without provocation, attacked an opera singer.

'So you managed to come,' he said. 'It's quite like sitting with myself when young, sitting with you, if you'll forgive me for saying so. I recognize you. I float upwards. I almost soar. You and I are entirely right about late Titian. No question. Great artists in old age are pristine, hopeful, inspired, full of bounteous surprises. No, they don't go stumbling along from thought to thought like the rest of us. In them the conscious and subconscious run ahead in ecstasy, by instinct. Probably they didn't even know what instinct was. Perhaps they were perplexed by their own mentality, curious to watch what would transpire. But one thing leads to another in paint. Oh, how one thing leads to another! That's what real painting is. Imagine it. Titian felt an essential truth quite close. He must have known it was standing next to him while he slept, must have felt on the very brink of painting the masterpiece he remembered imagining when young. By the time he was almost 90 he knew that facts pile up endlessly. You pile them up but they will not necessarily turn out to be true. The truth, if it's anywhere, may well be concealed in rhythms, pauses and flows. And, the chances are, when it finally makes its appearance it will be perfectly simple, incidental, the miraculous by-product of exuberance. Even of accident.'

Now, I told myself, I was really beginning to learn something, something I might remember, something I might well not hear again.

No doubt he kept himself well up on pills and alcohol but it did not take much to get Georges Idris started. Like a zoo animal, his imagination needed to be thrown raw meat, and I was it. He felt that in me he was holding forth to his younger self. All the reading and looking had finally paid off. He had seen the point of it, and now there was no containing him. I saw in front of me an old man in the grip of a bout of ecstasy, redolent with feeling, and it was a fine sight, if embarrassing.

He went on: 'Titian wasn't dealing in appearances. He didn't ape the form. He *implied* it. He knew exactly how we see, so his painting – by the time he was old – was a matter of *becoming* rather than being. In dealing with ambiguities he dealt with the divine. So why *should* he finish? What does he say about life, about death, in that last great, black and simultaneously blinding-bright *Pietà*? What does he say? I'll tell you. *Nothing*.'

'Nothing?'

'He has no need to. It is *we* who supply the meaning.'

And so, in this vein, Georges Idris continued through lunch and right through the afternoon. The waitress, slapping down in front of him his plate of risi-bisi, laughed and said, 'Control yourself'. In talking about life he went on very cheerfully to talk about death. He was onto death. He loved its vast perspectives, its way of dwarfing all that is of no importance.

'I can't do in old age what Titian did, but the remission of difficulties makes me happy. It doesn't matter a jot. It's a kindness of Venice to let me see what he saw. Titian's young grand-daughter, her beautiful face, turned and glanced at me out of the Pesaro altarpiece in the Frari only yesterday, just as she did at her grandfather. Some things, some places and pictures last, are not touched by change. There is much to encourage the illusion. It is we who eventually change and perish.'

At last we walked back to the Pensione Seguso, where Nils was waiting for him. 'Nils is obsessed with tarot cards,' he told me. 'He says they are not so much individual cards as a divided narrative. He makes his own.'

'It would have been conceivable,' Nils said.

I left Georges Idris in high spirits.

'When the water goes down in the morning we will brave the Piazzetta, you and I. Hot chocolate under the heavy awnings of Sansovino's library façade, begun 1537. Very long, unbroken façade. Caffè tables block the portico. Great richness of light and shade,' he said, smiling and waving as I took my leave.

Next day I got up early and, before my appointment with Georges Idris, went to find Titian, or at least where Titian had been. In a way I had got the two old men muddled up. The warps screamed horribly as they came tight at each landing stage when I made my way up the Grand Canal by vaporetto to Cà d'Oro. It was not much of a day, the sort of day Canaletto used to paint before he began to glitter for the tourists. Refuse-barges bumped up and down on grey water.

Aside from hearing his views on painting and much else, I had learned something of Idris himself. Well known as a painter in his thirties, with his own brand of Modernism, he had long been marginalized. He had a vitriolic hatred and contempt for the critic Albert Boizot, who had, in his view, assassinated his reputation almost single-handedly. Boizot seems to have seen through his borrowings. Montaigne was of the opinion that you should conceal everything you have been aided by and show only what you have done with it. Boizot considered Idris a plagiarist. Idris, blind to the fact that he and his Modernism were obsolete, felt himself now to be at the very top of his powers. Far from noticing that he was small beer, he had become increasingly elated. He was, he said, more energetic, more full of insights than ever. He, like Titian, was benefiting from 20 years of astounding, miraculous, God-given, late power. As he saw it, he had transcended taste and transcended his period. He did not volunteer to show me his recent work – he said he kept a studio in Calle dei Frati – but I was more than prepared to concede that he had a point. When he said that much new art was phony, a publicity stunt, and that he hated prizes, I agreed with him. Perhaps, in the canon of his sacred Modernism, he was of more than passing interest. Worth keeping. That was why a university museum still felt the need of his life-mask. And there was certainly no denying that, even if he was now something of a period piece, he had become a great talker.

All this was going round in my head as I made my way into a confusing and unfamiliar part of Venice up towards the Biri Grande. It had once been an aristocratic area but had been built on in a haphazard, unplanned way in the 19th century, extending it towards moorings on the Fondamenta Nuova. It had become run down. Here Titian had his palace and garden, and his studio to which the most important sitters in Europe came for more than 40 years. From here he had a view of the Alps. Lost, I eventually came on a courtyard called Campo del Titiano, but of its former grandeur nothing remained. It was full of rubbish. There was no longer any view.

Often you meet your destiny on the very road you take to avoid it.

Sensing there was something wrong, I hurried straight to Idris's pensione. By now the tide was coming in again. In the hall of the Seguso, chairs had been stacked on the marble-topped table. Dirty water was 18 inches deep on the floor. Nils was perched on a writing-desk, impatiently awaiting my arrival. It was not the water that bothered him.

Upstairs I found Idris dead on his bed. His head was tilted back, his chest bare. He was half on and half off the bed, with one foot on the floor.

'He was calling out for you,' Nils said.

'For long?'

'Yes. For a long time. Had it not been otherwise.'

The two of us lifted Idris out of the attitude of Titian's dead Christ and laid him flat on the mattress, as though to make him more comfortable. A pillow under his head.

'Did you comfort him when he was dying?'

'No,' Nils said, regarding me from under the hat. 'I didn't comfort him. Had it not been entirely believable. It was you he wanted.'

I did not know this old man. He had mistaken me for someone else and thought that he was me. I could understand that he was dead but I could not understand that from now on, every day, he and I would not be able to sit talking together in the Piazzetta. At that dead caffè to which we never went.

'I suppose he gave you no message for me, when I didn't come?'

'Oh yes, he certainly sent you a message. But it was of no interest. Would that it were.'

'Tell me, you idiot.'

He grinned at my impatience, wiping his white hands up and down on his thighs.

Eventually he said, 'It was a torrent of nonsense about what it is to be human.'

So this was how I finally saw Death. It was, after all, a tall, mad, old man struck dumb, who had wanted to tell me something.

The tide was now up to the fourth step of the stairs. I left the pensione, avoiding the worst of the deep water by going through the kitchens at the back, and quickly returned to my room. I collected the equipment I needed for making the mask.

Georges Idris's room was a large one, occupying half the front of the pensione on the second floor. Tessera-ed floor, rudimentary baroque frieze round the top of the walls. Heavily carved armoire. Sizeable bed. Cloudy wall-sconces of Murano-glass droplets. Some books open on a red table. A tarnished gilt chair. A henge of pill bottles on the washstand in the corner. A black mirror. The calmness of objects.

I began to grease the face. Every detail needed to be carefully greased so that, when the time came, the wax mould would detach cleanly, without difficulty. I was inexperienced and knew very little about what I was doing. From time to time big ships passed extremely close to the windows. They seemed almost to be in the room. Their engines churned past. On board the ships, disjointed sentences – orders, imprecations – were being broadcast in Russian, each syllable clearly audible.

I thought: from the dead, if you feel the need, you can take a cutting, a figurative one, in the hope that something of theirs continues in you. From Georges Idris I would take no aridity, nothing dry. Colour. A mass of window openings in the centre of a façade. Light dazzling the lagoon. On a clear day, a distant view of the Alps.

But now his relinquished room was the repository of shadow, and I was aware that some things failed to take place. Now I will tell you what failed to take place. For one thing, there was no lightning blinking and flickering over the roofs of Giudecca opposite, beyond the deep channel. Nor did the bells of the city toll, starting with the half-muffled, clothy booming of the distant basilica, taken up by the cracked bells in far-flung, derelict campanili which, accelerating as their arcs shortened, hesitated, struck a last time and finally stopped for good. Neither of these things occurred.

Inevitably, when I tried to remove the mould from Georges Idris's face, at 4.39 p.m., it became a distressing struggle. Twice I thought I should have to give up. Nils watched but did not help. He said, 'Had the opportunity not arisen.'

The result, in the end, was much better than I could have hoped. Far from having death written all over it, the face turned out to be beautifully animated. When I returned to Paris and cast the head, I was astounded at how lifelike it was. It is worth going to see, though the museum has placed it rather high on the wall with the others. The effect is due to the mouth being open. Georges Idris seems to be talking. Caught in mid sentence.

5

During the time that I was studying architecture in Paris in my early twenties I lived in attic rooms at 9 Quai d'Anjou. I took to walking many of the high routes in the Alps and Pyrenees in summer, and this led naturally to climbing. I was egged on to climb by my friend Guillaume Claudel, a philosophy student who usually came with me. It started with a conversation we had when walking from Chamonix to Mont Cervin. Left to myself I would have been perfectly content to stay on high paths and view the summits from below, but Claudel must always be attacking them and encouraging me to do the same.

For a third time we took the train from Interlaken to Lauterbrunnen and spent ten days staying in the village close to where the long mare's-tail of the Staubbach Falls drops in slow motion off its ledge onto a pile of tufa at the foot of the cliff beside the churchyard. We started with some local climbs in superb weather and then went higher, first using the ratchet-railway to Wengen and then taking the path that comes out above the tree-line and goes on upwards with an enormous view of the Jungfrau and Mönch. By now it was mid June. Butterwort, globularia, coltsfoot, anemones and gentians were flowering and everywhere there was the smell of vanilla orchids.

We made for our favourite place, a small pension by itself on a ledge at 6,000 feet. The building was very simple. A little flat-faced grey house, it seemed to lean back against the rock, its dilapidated shutters opening onto a spectacular view of the blinding glacier across the valley.

On our way up I saw a figure in front of us whom I thought I recognized. I had seen him once in the station at Brig and again ahead of us on the path as we walked up from Wengernalp. He was alone and evidently going in front of us on our own journey.

'This is the second time I have seen that man,' I remarked.

'He was on the platform at Interlaken.'

'You saw his face?'

'No. His back-view looked familiar.'

'He must think we are following him.'

'I shouldn't think he even knows we're here.'

I would not have been surprised to find that he had arrived ahead of us when we reached our pension, but there were only two other guests, a woman and her odd-looking square-jawed child, an eight-year-old boy with the face of a cruel adult. I put the matter out of my mind.

The walking and climbing were better than they had ever

been. We were out on the mountains all day, and in the evenings when we were pleasantly tired I encouraged Claudel to tell me his ideas on philosophy and music. The altitude and mountain air were always making him recall poetry.

'Remember Goethe?' he kept saying.

> 'Willst du immer weiter schweifen?
> Sieh, das Gute liegt so nah.
> Lerne nur das Glück ergreifen,
> Denn das Glück ist immer da.'

(Are you going to ramble on forever? Look how close happiness is. Learn only to reach out to it, for it is always there.)

There was one high valley, approached only by a difficult path, to which we often went. It was directly beneath the glacier, the enormous wall of which stood along the whole of one side of it, leaking water down a black cliff in permanent shadow.

'The Sublime,' Claudel said, 'has to do with domination and the transcendent and is not subject to reason.' But the valley itself was full of wildflowers. There were gentians, mountain pansies, lady's slipper orchids, and yellow swallow-tailed butterflies, and birds that are only found above 5,000 feet, including the rare three-toed woodpecker and green citril finches. Despite its dark cliff, the valley lay open to the sun all day long. Down the middle of it wound a stream on its way to the Lauterbrunnental. Nobody seemed to go there but us. Even the cattle, which had been driven up for the summer grazing, remained at its southern end. The clonking of their bells was just audible in the distance beyond the ridge.

In this gently sloping and soporific place time hesitated, and I experienced the absurd conviction, the conviction of youth given me by the mountains, that I would live forever. To Claudel's annoyance I did nothing but dawdle and gape. One lifetime, I thought, was not long enough in which to take it in.

Sometimes I tried to draw the valley because drawing is a pretext for looking, but on our return to the pension I always threw my drawings away. Although I drew them with a full heart, the mountains and their splendour could not be conveyed by a line, and the attempt was pointless. What did it matter, in the gigantic scheme of things, what effects the view had on my miniscule and inconsequential psyche? I remember moments of inordinate happiness I had there, which I believed could never be dispelled, because I was nobody and I was going nowhere.

At nights the glacier was noisy. Its creaking and moaning were more noticeable than during the day, as if it was a restless sleeper in a neighbouring bed. Always in motion, it let fall fragments of rock and ice loosened by hot sun in the afternoons.

I suspect it was listening to this that began to make Claudel think of going across it.

'It's not difficult,' he said.

'Why can't we just admire it from here?'

'Ah, but we must cross it to get to the mountain.'

I had been afraid that this would happen. Claudel knew perfectly well that I was more than happy where I was, but he persisted.

'You can walk up it with your hands in your pockets,' he said. 'But we had better try it this month. If we leave it until July the joint between the glacier and the rock face will loosen and come undone in the sun. In weather as good as this it would be a pity not to try.'

The woman with the jut-jawed child was sitting outside on the bench in front of the pension, reading a German newspaper, and overheard our conversation.

'You should go,' she said.

'Well, I'm not doing it without a guide.'

'That's settled then,' said Claudel, smiling. 'I'll go down and get one tomorrow.'

The man he brought back next day was a French guide, born in Chamonix, well qualified according to his *carte*, who had undertaken the climb already several times that season and made light of it. He pointed out the route on the framed relief-map in the hall and then asked us to look across at the mountain.

'You see that notch there,' he said, 'the one above the moraine? There's a gentle traverse to be made across the face just above it. It's only a 40-degree slope and the snow is still firm there. The last part looks worse than it is.'

Instead of enjoying the mountain against the pure blue sky, as a breathless spectacle above its gigantic glittering foreground of glacier, I was already forced to see it in a new way as a succession of difficulties. Having looked at the summit off and on all day for weeks, I had thought I was familiar with it.

'Now look a little to the left of that arête. What do you see?'

'The face looks completely smooth to me,' Claudel said. The guide shook his head and handed him binoculars.

'Look closer.'

I took the binoculars from Claudel. As the rock-face below the summit came into focus, I could make out that it was composed of a series of shallow steps, hard to see from underneath.

'It's a staircase,' the guide said. 'The shelves tilt inwards and are mostly a metre deep.'

'Didn't I tell you?' Claudel said. 'You just walk up.'

'So you are going then?' the German woman said to me, and laughed. She took the cigarette from between her red lips and blew a long plume of smoke into the air. Her dark glasses were small and round, and behind their lenses her eyes seemed to be missing.

We roped up to cross the glacier. As the sun rose, the crevasses in the old ice showed their cerulean interiors. The guide went first. *'Il y a toujours quelque chose d'absent qui me tourmente,'* I said to myself.

The hardest part was getting across the bergschrund, the joint between the glacier and the mountain where the last of the compacted summer snow was beginning to break away, but once we were on the long moraine the going was easy and we made fast progress. Guillaume Claudel, who was normally talkative, became silent as we worked our way up the rock staircase and the astounding view began to have its effect. The clear air was stinging and exhilarating, and once we had crossed the last arête we felt the influence of a slight but distinct up-draught.

There was a difficult couloir, very steep, and then an overhanging lip of hard snow, a cornice along the crest of a ridge, which the guide broke through with care to avert a collapse.

Shortly after midday we stood on the summit. The panorama was stupendous. Away to the south-west in the far distance we could see three or four narrow columns of cloud which stuck up like sticks of celery. They reached high into the air and broadened out at the top. They were the first clouds we had seen for weeks.

'Summer thunderstorms,' the guide said.

His face was very white because of the protective grease he had put on. It occurred to both Claudel and me that he appeared to have the mask of a white-faced monkey.

In that infinitely dramatic, high place, Claudel leant towards me and whispered in my ear. 'Voltaire's monkey,' he said. *'Le singe estropié.'*

The guide rather quickly enumerated some of the many peaks and aiguilles in the view, and after a short rest we started the descent.

The staircase was harder to go down than up, and several times Claudel kicked rubble by mistake off the ledges. We watched it spin dizzily down the couloir, bound noisily off the rock-face and drop across the moraine.

'You should be more careful,' the guide said, angrily. He said it more than once. 'That is not a good idea. Move as fast as you can, but deliberately. With precision.'

It was late afternoon before we successfully made our way over the moraine. The kicked-down rubble and boulders had jumped and slid across it and damaged the fragile snow bridges between it and the glacier.

The place at which we had crossed on the way up had collapsed under the bombardment and we were forced to work our way along the snow-wall crabwise in search of a safe crossing point. It was not difficult to understand the guide's irritation at our carelessness. Beneath his white mask he was no longer in control of his temper.

'Disregard him,' I said to Claudel. 'It is dangerous to hurry.'

We spent half an hour looking for a safe bridge but did not find one.

The sun was going off our side of the mountain and we were already in shadow before we finally found a place which might do. It spanned the chasm but was extremely narrow, a rib or flying buttress made of rotting snow. Guillaume Claudel made his way safely across it by lying on his stomach and inching backwards, but, as he did so, large chunks of snow broke off from underneath and disappeared.

'I shall go next,' the guide shouted. 'Re-rope at once.' And he climbed down past me. 'You are idiots. Imbéciles.'

'Wait,' I said. 'Surely we must throw a rope to Guillaume on the lower side. If you slip I can't hold your weight from here. I haven't the grip.'

'Do as I say! Do as I say, damn you. Do as I say!' he yelled, hurriedly spreading his weight as gently and evenly as he could across the bridge and beginning to slide backwards across it.

For a moment the snow arch held, but then it became apparent that it was detaching from the lower side. It seemed to take a long time to collapse.

When the last of the bridge had fallen, the guide hung from the edge looking up at me, and I recognized his monkey-white face.

With the terrible effort of clinging to the lip of the crevasse, his features were distorted into what appeared to be a derisive grin. His goggles had been knocked sideways and I could see that his eyes were full of hatred. One of them, the left eye, turned inwards in a squint.

I made no attempt to help him. And, in the moments before he fell into the abyss, I recognized that he was me.

6

When they let me out of hospital there was a heat wave in Paris, and trouble in the streets.

I told no one, not even Guillaume Claudel, that I had recognized the guide. But because none of us is wholly rational I went to confession and half told the priest.

I knelt in the confessional and waited in the gloom.

'Expiation or outer darkness,' the old voice said.

'I have allowed a man to die, Monsieur le Curé.'

'In what way?'

'I did nothing to save him.'

'And you feel guilt?'

'I do, Monsieur le Curé.' I kept silent, kneeling in the darkness.

'Do you know what guilt is?' He answered his own question. 'The crux of guilt is: was avoidable wrong done?'

'It was, Monsieur le Curé.'

'Disowning guilt damages the immortal soul.'

'I cannot disown it.'

There was a long pause during which he seemed to be sleeping. Then he said, 'You have allowed your brother to die.'

I knew he meant my brother in Christ, but I realized at once that this was how I would think of the dead man. I would think of him as my dead twin brother, the part of myself I had refused to save.

'There is forgiveness if you feel guilt. The damage is not irreparable. Guilt requires remorse and expiation.'

'But what is forgiveness, Monsieur le Curé?'

'Forgiveness is simple,' he replied. 'It is a refusal to blame.'

Again he kept silent and so did I. Then I heard him wiping the saliva from his lips with a handkerchief before he added quietly, with his face close to the grille, 'And there is nothing that may not be forgiven.'

7

With the arrival of the *fermeture annuelle* the city emptied. August was suffocatingly hot. Offices closed. From the street you could hear telephones ringing in empty buildings. There was a transport strike and then a refuse-collection strike.

I took to going to the cinema in the afternoons.

There was a semi-derelict art house that I knew of in the Marais which was still working. It smelled of sweat and cigarettes but the flickering dark was consoling and the images took me out of myself. The films, though obscure, were good and I began to realise a state of mind that has recurred at various stages in my life: an appetite, a readiness for something exceptional, something to which I could attach myself and which I could pursue with total conviction.

Most afternoons I would get out of the beating sunlight, buy my *billet* from the Algerian in the glass booth, who had a tube up his nose to help him breathe, and feel my way to a seat. There were never more than two or three other people there and I did not see their faces because they sat behind me. Sometimes they made disparaging comments to each other or to the actresses on the screen and sometimes they got some sleep. If the film kept them awake or was not to their liking – or had anything to do with Surrealism – they cut up rough and voted noisily with their feet, saying that films revolted them anyway. But, despite disgusting its clientele on a regular basis, the cinema was stubbornly loyal to the experimental.

One day I was late and, as I settled in the gloom, I assumed they were showing an old newsreel with a French soundtrack. Hairs vibrated in the corners of the frame and disappeared. Numbers came and went. The splotched black and white film showed Madrid from a succession of high windows. In the streets were cars with mattresses tied to their roofs as protection against snipers. The scene was set in the July that Franco and his Moroccan troops were on their way to occupying Salamanca and Burgos. The communists were liberating political prisoners and the Confederacion National de Trabajo was beginning its executions. Spanish refugees were being picked up at the French border and put into camps.

And then the narrative, which was part news-story and part fiction, seemed to fragment. Like a collection of short stories which has been shuffled, it consisted of hypnotically beautiful segments, episodes at different levels, some of reality and some of imagination. Past and future were shown next to one another. Sequences were incomplete and the narrative would stop and re-start as if the director had forgotten what it was he intended to say and needed to re-state and re-remember what he had first thought of. It was cut as though much of it was missing and other quite minor incidents had been re-arranged and amplified. It was not realistic but had the exactness of recollection. I was reminded of the look of outlandishness I had noticed in the mountain landscape as Claudel and I walked up from Wengernalp, the look of absolute outlandishness that is characteristic of a real place. The film existed in a limbo, a location re-remembered in which faces and images from the past could meet.

It was showing for a fortnight and I saw it each day until I had learned every frame. It provided me with something I had always hoped to find in film and never seen before.

I became addicted to it.

No one knew anything about it. There was no sign of it in the French National Film Archive or in the Prague index. The Film Institute had no print. The owner of the Paris cinema sent a message to say that the film had been loaned to him by the Czech Film Institute and that, according to them, all other prints had been bought up long ago by Paramount and destroyed for their silver nitrate content. Nothing was known about the director, Krzysztof Cviic. 'Probably not his real name,' said a man who was standing in the shadow at the back of the cinema's glass ticket-booth so that I could only see his feet. He was wearing bright yellow shoes.

Apart from Cviic's there were nine other names on the list of credits. I wrote them on the wall of my apartment and set about tracking people down.

'I have to find the director,' I told Claudel, who was again in the mountains.

'It sounds as if it's the film of a dream,' Claudel said. 'You know that Buñuel dreamed most of *Le Chien Andalou*.'

'This has nothing to do with Surrealism.'

'The trill in Tartini's *Devil's Trill* violin sonata is supposed to have been dreamed. He woke up and simply wrote it down.'

'This isn't a film of a dream. It's rational, practically a documentary. Something absent or half remembered. I'm sure it's autobiographical.'

'Well, time plays odd tricks with film. You never quite know which tense you are in.'

The heat was still intense. The sky seemed to sag under its burden of smoke. Tarmac was soft, the river torpid. Women in aprons, queuing in the sun for groceries, knitted standing up. A long barge, loaded with sand, was having difficulty with the current. It passed laboriously into and then out of the shadow under a bridge. A skeletal, blind accordion player was ignored by a group of postal workers who sat on the curb, smoking and tilting a wine bottle. But the film worked against inertia.

After several days on the phone I traced the female lead, who called herself Mona Manzoni, to an experimental school in Vermont.

'Do you have someone on your staff called Mona Manzoni?'

'He isn't here.'

'No. A woman. Miss Mona Manzoni.'

'It's a terrible line. I'm just the janitor. Manny, do we have anyone here called ___? What did you say the name was?'

A different voice said 'Who is this?'

'I'm trying to contact a Miss Mona Manzoni.'

'Are you joking?'

'Why?'

'I've just been consulting my deputy here but he can't recall.'

'She's an actress. Mona Manzoni is probably her film name.'

'Movies?'

There was the sound of a slight scuffle and the voice of the janitor came on again.

'Sure we had a teacher here called herself that. Went around acting all day long. No one listened to her. She hated children.'

'Do you know where she is now?'

'The forwarding address I have here is Lyndonville.'

I wrote down the address he gave me with extreme care. My electric fan, hunting for air, turned from side to side as though slowly shaking its head in disbelief.

At the end of the week I went to America to find her.

★

Mona Manzoni in the film was an androgynous blond boy who had a habit of sitting forward with her arms dangling between her legs and then rocking backwards to laugh in an apparently carefree way, usually in close-up. But in order to meet her I crossed several time zones, and so had she. Only her film-self belonged in the continuous present, and the 'cello-like voice.

She had on a cream and white dress and her hair was up but she seemed to be wearing her psyche inside out. As architecture she looked like the New York Guggenheim. She was eager to talk about the film and especially about herself and Krzysztof Cviic but it soon turned out that she was nursing the kind of grievance which requires maintenance and she was looking for support.

'It's a responsibility being someone's muse. Krzysztof Cviic was obsessed with me. The difficulty was that he never told me exactly what it was he wanted from my acting. Well, he explained to me how to behave more or less naturally in front of the camera. According to him, I was just to be an unhurried version of myself. But very soon all that did was make me realise I had practically no idea of who I was in the first place. It soon became obvious to me that, in order to be myself, I needed to re-invent myself as someone else entirely. It was as if he was making me stand in for someone who had nothing to do with me. That isn't me you see in the picture. It's someone I became unknowingly because of him and the camera.' While she said this she was peeling an apple. She peeled it in one long unbroken spiral which dangled down.

'To tell you the truth, at the time I had very little idea what was going on. None of us did. There was no proper script. I think Krzysztof kept us deliberately in the dark. He kept telling me I was the reason for the movie, its subject and inspiration, and that I was indispensable. I don't know why I looked as I did. He said I was metaphysical. It's all in close-ups because he was unable to take his eyes off me. He couldn't work or live without me, even for a moment.'

She smiled at me in close-up and I saw that she was crying.

'And what does metaphysical mean in that context anyway? I couldn't help being the age I was, of seeming to be the person I was, and I had absolutely no control over how I came across on screen.'

Part of her hair had come down. She began to eat the peel and not the apple.

'In fact I had no control over how I came across in life. The screen altered me into someone who didn't exist. I became a stranger to myself. I haven't felt complete since. I am worn out with dreaming.'

When she said that, she looked infinitely more beautiful than she ever had in the film but I could not tell if she was acting.

She placed her hands on the small of her back, and stretched. She said, 'Now I begin to ache. What was always perfect and always praised, my body, is no longer perfect and even begins to be ugly. What before was beautiful is now spoilt and becomes a burden. I bruise easily. My smile is of regret. I had not expected life to be like this so soon or so unreservedly.'

Then she pulled herself together.

'You know about the ancient world?' she asked.

'Yes. Why?'

'Lollius Bassus. Recommended reading for all muses.'

And, her face wet with tears, she quoted as follows:

'I refuse to become a shower of gold,
A bull or a swan as in days of old.
Let Zeus do tricks. Corinna's more willing
If I remain human and give her a shilling.'

She made a doomed attempt to put her hair up again.

'I just want to be myself,' she said, 'and the bastards make me into everyone else.'

'But to be the *raison d'être* for a picture as good as that,' I said, 'even half as good, isn't negligible, is it?'

'Even if nobody looks at it now?'

'At the end, why did you say, in English "And don't forget to thank your mother for the rabbit"?'

'Oh, Krzysztof made me say that on the spur of the moment. He said he could smell the vowels.'

8

Mona Manzoni did not know where Krzysztof Cviic was but she could put me in touch with the film's cameraman, who lived on the Massachusetts coast.

'Come and look,' he said when I got there. 'There's something wrong with the sea.'

At the back of his house the water was wallowing and guzzling unpleasantly against the steps of the deck. In the blinding sun the white wall of a lighthouse down the coast made a bright curve like a full sail. Some big yachts, reefed and with their lee rails under, exposed their expensive varnished keels in the swell. In the distance, out beyond the islands, great humps of water were chasing each other along like moving boils.

I put my hand in the water. It was unnaturally hot.

When we went into the house the storm doors rattled little and often as the sea breeze picked at them. Art Otterbach was in a wheelchair. A stroke. On its rubber wheels the chair moved him quickly and smoothly about as if it were a camera-dolly.

He brought his face round from the sea onto me and focused. I could tell that he did not at all like what he saw.

'If you want to know about the film and Krzysztof, I'll tell you, but I don't believe you'll understand a word I say.

'The point is that Krzysztof distrusts art. He knows that structure and significance, which are essential to any work of art, are utterly absent from life. Life is lived in small and ordinary moments which have no story to tell, and lives are filled with random events which shape them. Chance is the greatest story teller. Isn't that Balzac?

'That doesn't mean the picture isn't rigorously composed. What seems a chaotic process of back-tracking, recopying, striking out, tacking on and amplifying is exactly the process of recollection. Nothing exists until it is remembered. If he sometimes filmed ideas in no particular order it was because he needed to catch them before he forgot them. And while Krzysztof had film and money he used them. He was like a letter-writer who runs out of space and continues up the margins and onto the envelope.

'The film doesn't end. Its revisions simply break off incomplete. The implication is that it flows out of sight. Revisions could continue indefinitely or else the whole film could be repeated with perfect logic, which is the same implication that you find in Proust. You know about *l'ironie Proustienne?*'

I said I did and hoped for the best. Outside, shreds of unhealthy looking cloud the colour of verdigris were being driven along high up and at tremendous speed. In another room I could hear an old record of 'Body and Soul', the part in which the tenor saxophone plays the melody at half the speed of the rest of the band but the two lines fit together flawlessly.

'Do you have a photograph of Krzysztof Cviic?' I asked.

'Yes. It's on the wall behind you.'

When I turned round, all I could see was a framed colour photograph of a townscape.

'It looks like a film set,' I said.

'No. It's Livingstone, Montana,' he said. 'Last summer.'

'But Krzysztof Cviic?'

The photograph showed an intersection. The main street had only one side because the railway ran parallel next to it. There was a train approaching from far away. Pool rooms and diners with false fronts seemed closed. There were many overhead wires radiating at each crossing. In the middle distance there was a grain silo. At the end of each street there were distant mountains. It looked hot. Midday. There were no people on the sidewalks and there was no traffic except for an old Dodge pickup with a dog standing in the back of it, which was describing a wide arc in the dust at the intersection.

'I meant a picture of Krzysztof Cviic,' I said. And then I looked more closely and saw that, very small, in the lower right-hand corner there was a solitary figure in a wide hat, standing on his short shadow, his back to the camera.

'Yes, that's him,' Art Otterbach said. 'You can't see them in the picture but he was wearing the eccentric yellow shoes that Zazou sold him.'

'Yellow shoes?'

'That's right. It's a silent picture, isn't it? The silence of noon. Appropriate because Krzysztof is deaf.'

And then I noticed that Krzysztof Cviic had his arms raised slightly in the air as if signing. Because he had his back to the camera, it was impossible to read the sign. But then I looked at his shadow, and the sign was plain enough on the ground. He was signing 'Doubles'.

*

All the furniture in Art Otterbach's house was sticky with sea salt. In the sea breeze the muslin curtains curled lazily into the rooms. The salt had adhered for years to the wood-shingled roof and walls, turning them silver.

The next day, Zazou and I went sailing.

Zazou was Art Otterbach's companion. When he was not looking after Art he worked in the Emerald Shoe Shop, in Mattapoisett. He was a handsome man in his fifties with a brown face and watery eyes. When I met him he looked at me sharply, was going to say something and then I saw him change his mind. He smiled to himself as if at a private joke.

At first we sailed without speaking. The confused sea had settled down but there was still a stiff breeze. As we made our way out, a single cloud cast a patch of shadow on the water where a bell-buoy swung indolently in the swell, and the only other sounds were of the runneling water against the keel and the occasional creak of the stay sail and missen.

'There is always a skeleton in the buffet,' Zazou said, looking thoughtfully at the coast as we turned east past the lighthouse. 'All that fattens is not soft.'

I watched him to see if he was quoting but he betrayed no hint of this and remained perfectly serious. Nor did the sea have even the shadow of grammar on it.

'The sea interrogates its beaches secretly,' he went on. 'Thick waters stifle in furs. The vol-au-vent and the wind his valet.'

I did not reply but waited to find out what would happen, imagining the silver-splashed wall of his brain, and his subconscious, murky like the bottom of the sea.

The boat was a ketch and difficult to work. It carried a jib, a stay sail and as well as the mainsail there were a topsail and missen. Zazou's skill with all these was astonishing, but apart from an occasional upward glance into the rigging he began constantly staring over the side into the deep water as if keeping a lookout for something.

'Come and hear the strident cry of red eggs,' he said suddenly, and I saw that he was taking the catch off a winch at the stern that let out a trawl-net. There were davits.

When the net had sunk and was fully out I took the helm and we continued along the coast for two hours in the sun, the ketch on a peaceful broad reach above its reflection in the packed cosmos. In the distance gannets were crash-diving for fish.

Then there was a jolt and the boat was retarded by a weight.

'Now,' said Zazou, looking down into the net, 'make way for the banal machinery of despair,' and we began to winch in. The ratcheting became harder. As the net swung dripping onto the davits we had our first sight of what hung so heavily constricted in the mesh, and then the creature lay in the bottom of the boat: a gigantic conger eel.

Zazou put his head down close to it and looked into its eyes. Its eyes were puffy like a boxer's. It stared back at him at short range. There was a pulse visible behind its flattened skull. The long tube of its body was like a leg swollen by a terrible thrombosis. Its skin was black crepe. It did not struggle.

We turned back. I worked the sails and the helm, and Zazou did not for a moment take his eyes off those of the eel.

On the dock in the town there was a small aquarium converted from an old fish-salting building, a blockhouse, opposite which the fishing boats tied up.

The eel, accustomed to living in 150 metres of water, was accommodated in a concrete trench not much more than a metre deep which had previously been the live-bait tank and which ran along two sides of the aquarium's single room. The creature lay without moving and was unable to turn round. The room was kept in semi-darkness except for lit-up tanks around the edge. Zazou refused to leave the eel but sat on a wooden chair near its head. The room was stone cold. I brought him rugs.

I described to Art Otterbach what had happened.

'Zazou seems to be having difficulty breathing,' I said.

All that night we waited for him to come home.

'You must take me to him,' Art Otterbach said at last. So before it was properly light I pushed him in his wheelchair to the aquarium, long before anyone was about. When we went into the darkened room, all I could hear was Zazou's breathing. At first I thought it was the oxygen system of the fish tanks.

He was suffocating. His shoulders were drawn up and his throat made the coughing sound of forced air. There were moments when, seeming about to lose consciousness, he struggled to the surface again in a panic as though terrified of drowning. The immense eel lay motionless in its trench, staring at him.

In one of the lit tanks a ray, like a nun with a hair lip, opened its white vestments and moved leisurely upwards against the glass. In others, cuttle-fish hung among stirred particles, their small elephant heads with dangling tubes blowing them backwards. Turbots lay in the gravel with mouths on the sides of their faces and marbles for eyes. Lobsters, which prey on each other and can taste with their feet, felt into caves with their antennae to check if they were occupied.

When I positioned Art Otterbach's wheelchair next to Zazou he sat with him for ten minutes, listening to him struggling for breath. Then he reached over and put his hand on Zazou's arm.

'It is quite simple,' he said. 'You must put the eel back.'

Under engine now, we took the eel along the coast later that same day to the point where I estimated it to have been caught. Although the water was glittering, I saw the sea as a ribbon of black appearing and disappearing at differing levels beside us.

When we stopped and drifted there was silence except for the knocking of a rope, the tapping of a stay. And when I looked at Zazou he seemed to have stopped breathing altogether. As quickly as possible I winched the eel over the side into the water. Zazou and the eel still did not take their eyes off one another, and for what seemed a long time it remained where it was without moving.

Then it suddenly reversed strongly out of the net and wagged powerfully down into the deep water, out of sight among the enormous submerged cliffs and drowned mountains. And we returned to our puny port.

Although Zazou could now breathe, he began a period of mourning.

When, after a few days, he disappeared, I went to look for him at the Emerald Shoe Shop. That summer the shop was full of sling backs and silver mules with raffia flowers, and in the window were gold sandals with spaghetti straps and shoes made of fuchsia imitation snakeskin. But Zazou was not there.

I ran to the aquarium. He was lying fully clothed in what had been the eel's trench, floating on his back.

'Zazou!' I made a grab for him. But he held up a hand and said in a strong voice:
'The crayfish has the bestial voice of a raspberry.
'The hair of the fruitful years stands on end but the water remains empty.
'Even the lemon falls to its knees before the beauty of nature.
'Alas, our good Kaspar is dead.
'Who will blow the noses of ships' umbrellas now and bore the pyramids?
'And who will interpret for us the monograms in the stars?'

9

As soon as I reached Paris I went to find Krzysztof Cviic, but the cinema was boarded up, disfigured and partly vandalized. I eventually located the Algerian who had worked in the box office. He was out of a job and he had no information. He had no idea even of Cviic's identity, let alone his whereabouts.

It rained every day. The Seine was yellow with gravel washed down from the gravel-banks near Rouen. I returned to my architectural studies.

My father kept me waiting when I went to see him.

For half an hour I sat in the outer office. Under a cruel strip light, his morose typist told me about her twins while painting her nails. Her face, hands and arms were freckled with punctuation marks the colour of melted Demerara sugar. When she crossed her legs I saw that her calves sported constellations of asterisks.

Then she said 'How am I?' as though she knew I had been staring. There was a noise on her desk, and I went through into the main office.

My father looked frantic. When he finally put the telephone receiver back on its cradle, I said something quite different from the speech I had prepared. Forgetting that he loathed to be touched and regarded any bodily contact as a repulsive and unforgivable assault, I grasped him by the wrists and in a voice I hardly recognized as my own I told him that I could no longer remember who I was.

'Let go of me,' he said ferociously, disconnecting my grip. 'And t-try to be rational.'

When he was annoyed he had a minor speech impediment on certain diphthongs.

Instead of addressing my problem he passed me a piece of paper on which was scrawled most, but not all, of the following equation:

$$z(\zeta) = A + B \int^{\zeta} S_B(\zeta') \prod_{k=1}^{n_0} [\omega(\zeta', a_k^{(0)})]^{\beta_k^{(0)}} \prod_{j=1}^{M} \prod_{k=1}^{n_j} [\omega(\zeta', a_k^{(j)})]^{\beta_k^{(j)}} d\zeta'$$

with

$$S_B(\zeta) \equiv \left(\frac{\omega_\zeta(\zeta, \alpha)\omega(\zeta, \bar{\alpha}^{-1}) - \omega_\zeta(\zeta, \bar{\alpha}^{-1})\omega(\zeta, \alpha)}{\prod_{j=1}^{M} \omega(\zeta, \gamma_1^{(j)})\omega(\zeta, \gamma_2^{(j)})} \right)$$

While I read it he rubbed the sides of his head, which made his hair stand on end.

He said, 'Three times in the last week I have dreamed about this equation. It is known as the Schwarz-Christoffel equation. It was invented in the 1860s but has never been completed. If it were, it would enable engineers to work out the m-maximum stress tolerated by buildings made of drilled-out shapes. It would revolutionize bridge design. It is a famous, long-running, unsolved mathematical problem.'

'I have heard of it.'

'There. Even you have heard of it. My dreams about it are totally lacking in logic. I dream that, with outlandish irrationality, I apply the theory of Schottley groups to the problem instead of using conventional mathematics, and I solve it. I s-solve it! Each time I wake up I write out as much of the solution to the problem as I can remember. But each time there is only so much of it I can recall. It is driving me mad.'

'You mean it is not finished?'

'Not finished.' He put his fingers together in the shape of a bridge and made a cracking noise with the joints.

'Supposing you don't dream it again,' I said spitefully, 'or supposing you dream it but can't remember it?'

'It's worse than that,' he said. 'I can n-now n-no longer go to sleep at all.'

★

At the time I graduated I had no real idea of what was going on, but nor had anybody else.

Guillaume Claudel and his friends had become Communists. The first Mao posters began to appear in the Sorbonne. My copine, Laure, dressed in bizarre fashion and black leather jacket, complained constantly about '*les flics féroces*' and scribbled on the walls in streets off Boulevard Saint-Michel 'It is forbidden to forbid' and '*Sous les pavés, la plage*'.

Despite all this, the economy was booming and my father's civil engineering firm was being awarded ever larger government contracts. And then there was another in the long series of miners' strikes. My cousin Alain, at Nanterre, went off to work for Chirac. In Paris there were non-stop protests.

Laure and I had a particular form of student attachment. We had manipulated our college photograph. By standing at the edge of the massed ranks and, as the camera slowly tracked, running fast along the back of the group, we had succeeded in positioning ourselves in the nick of time at the opposite end as well. It had worked perfectly. In the final print, on either side of the rows of faces, there we were. With a look of absolute conviction, we appeared twice.

'So you are abandoning Tante Yvonne,' Laure said, laughing, when I told her I was going to Greece on a post-graduate scholarship, 'and the fossilized mechanisms of the world.'

When she came to the station to see me off, she said, 'What the gods most love is some quite ordinary misapprehension.'

She said this just as the train began to move.

'What?' I shouted, but she only smiled and waved as she

diminished in size, and, though she called out what might have been an explanation, I could not hear her.

10

Greek temples looked to me as though they were not so much ruins as still in the process of construction. The boat from Piraeus, a re-fitted Turkish merchant ship, had no sense of urgency, smelled of hot oil and made prodigious amounts of smoke. Manual workers returning to the islands from their jobs in the cities slept against the lifeboats and ventilators in the sun. We progressed extremely slowly past Delos and Mikonos.

The only person in motion on the ship was a monk with kapélo, beard and pigtail who walked constantly round the deck. Each time he passed, re-appearing from behind the deckhouse and picking his way, he smiled at me. He stopped to talk, and soon afterwards a second monk went by. I realized I had been watching two identical monks and mistaken them for one.

'Could I borrow a cigarette?' he said in French. He looked at me, eyes narrowed through the smoke. Behind him the Aegean was ultramarine, indigo, cerulean, phthalo and azure, all at the same time.

'You haven't such a thing as a drink, have you?' he asked. 'On the island, fresh water is delivered only once a week'.

When he had drunk the beer I gave him, he asked if I could spare another.

'I work at Ioanni Tou Theologou,' he said. 'You may call me Papantonis.' He shook me gratefully by the hand. His smiling face was the bitumen-ink colour of a patriarch on a Greek banknote.

'It is a very slow ship,' he said. 'Would you like to play bezique to pass the time? Or piquet? Of course, as Godot knows, if we do not play, the time will pass anyway. Why not see what cards fortune allots you at whist? You can always call *misére* or *misére ouvert* at that. We will invite these two people to play with us. It is not the cards that are sinners but men.'

He dealt the cards next to his long sandals on the deck, where we sat against the rail.

'We will know when we approach the island from the smell.'

'Fish?'

'Fish, yes, but also thyme, eucalyptus, acacia and wild sage after the day's heat.'

He played most enjoyably, talking all the time.

'We are gambling against all men's enemy, chance,' he said. 'Do you know klabberjass? It is like pichet but Dutch. You played the trey. You think you have free will, but God knows what you will do.'

'Even at cards?'

'Of course.'

'You think I am fated to lose?'

'We follow our natural urges, even at cards.'

Each time we paused in our playing, he returned to his beads. He won a few drachmas.

'You have to sense the significance of each card,' he said, 'know it by intuition.'

'Teach me.'

'What did you say?'

'Teach me.'

'There is nothing I would rather do. You can tell me about Diderot and I will tell you about Plato and Christ, and in the process you might improve at cards, the devil's books. Could you spare another cigarette?'

'Is it determined that you have one?'

He lit it and, speaking through the smoke said, 'Apparently yes, but memory and the mind are a book which writes itself.'

We were playing demon with so much concentration that we failed to notice the smell of the island. The ship backed up to the quay. For a moment, with a shock, I thought I saw Zazou in the crowd. He was seated at a table, playing chess. But he was playing blindfolded. When I disembarked he was no longer there. His chair was occupied by a much older man who looked nothing like him, and I concluded that I had been mistaken.

By the time our departed ship was a smudge of black smoke on the horizon, Papantonis had arranged for me to a hire a room. He took me to a barber's shop. A sign read *Koypeion Kpinos xpiz Koymen Aoypoy.*

The barber unhurriedly wiped the soap off his razor onto a piece of brown paper, balanced the long blade across a cup of hot water, left a customer under a sheet as if dead, and slowly showed me a room next door which belonged to him. It was a tall room, empty except for a bed and a chair. It cost next to nothing. It was above the Arion bar, and its window overlooked the town square. I rented it for two weeks, and Papantonis left on his *teuf-teuf*, going up the hill to his monastery.

While I was buying him a tsipouro in the Arion bar next day, he said, 'You know, what you need is to stay here for the rest of the summer. Abandon your studies. The whole purpose of youth is to fritter it away. Why not gravely interrupt death with pleasure? In the process you might learn something.'

'You mean I can choose?'

'Oh yes, you have a choice. You even have the freedom to argue and reason. The gods were created by ignorance and fear and are worshipped by credulity.'

'But you say I have no free will.'

'Feelings too are indispensable, and you can always hope.'

He dealt the cards. 'Today I thought black lady hearts. It is like whist. Will you stay?'

'Of course I'll stay.'

'Good.'

'I have no choice.'

'You are learning, and a touch of the sun is a valid excuse for most things. I couldn't borrow a Karelia, could I?'

Someone was playing repeated fourths on a zither.

★

Each day the sun seemed not to make much progress.

I spent my time in the sea and on the beach. My skin became the black-bronze colour of ancient coins and, without trying,

I developed the athletic body of Greek sculpture. Quite soon I hardly recognized myself. The sea provided total gratification. I lived among decaying dynasties with a sense of new wellbeing, and most evenings Papantonis took a meal or some money off me in exchange for my Greek education.

'A bet on a game of cards brings hope into lives which would otherwise be without it,' he said. 'And I do not prize my time so greatly that I cannot spend a good part of most days doing my best to combat the tedium of ordinary life.'

He seemed incapable of eating without getting food all over himself.

'The ancient Greeks invented vowels,' he said, while eating feta cheese, olives and tomatoes as he always did. Table manners were something to which he was a stranger. 'The only ancient Greek music known is in 5/4 time.'

Or, 'Did you know that hypocrite was the old Greek word for actor?'

'I know that Flaubert visited the Parthenon.'

'Really.'

'Yes.'

Papantonis said, 'Today we will play with Italian cards. In Italy packs have fifty cards, aubergines are clubs, then cups, swords and suns.'

He must have thought that to me he seemed old. One day he quoted Euripides, as follows:

'Alas, how right the ancient saying is: We, who are old, are nothing else but noise and shape. Like mimicries of dreams we go, and have no wits, although we think us wise.'

He leaned back in his chair and picked his teeth.

'Voltaire says you should judge a man by the questions he asks.'

Papantonis laughed. 'How about some baklava with extra honey and a game of canasta with friends, or California loo?'

I passed the whole of August, the dog days, on the beach. Day after day I experienced pleasures of the body that were so seductive they put an end to thought. I forgot everything except the sea and the sun, and my own well-being. Time meant nothing to me. The idea of hell was inconceivable.

'You said you would tell me about rhetoric,' I reminded Papantonis one evening in the Arion.

'Rhetoric will keep,' he said. 'You see those people over there?'

'Yes. Americans off the Poseidon ferry?'

'Americans, but off a yacht.'

'Do you know them?'

'No, but I have seen them playing cards.'

'You feel we need some competition?'

'I think by now you and I have developed a rapport. Even at fan tan we could withstand some stiffer opposition.'

'You mean much higher stakes?'

'Well,' he said. 'We could at least see what cards the devil allots us in the bodies of lost souls. Or do you think that would be to risk the blackest pits of vile foulness?'

The American couple turned out to be people who have one character in normal life and a completely different one at the card table. Away from cards they were backslapping and convivial, but as soon as they had cards in their hands they were silent, humourless, unblinking, and as dangerous as snakes.

For five nights we lost to them, and each game cost me an inordinate amount of money.

'You may lose all your money,' Papantonis said, 'but that is nothing compared to the damage done by yourself to yourself if you lead an unjust life.'

'Plato?'

'Plato certainly thinks injustice harms the doer. The unjust man, he says, is the most miserable of all creatures.'

'Yes, but what has that to do with cards?'

'If you lend me another Karelia I will tell you.' He leaned forward across the table.

'First, try to remember that the general rule for a long shot to become an even-money chance is to multiply the odds by 0.69, for practical purposes 0.7.'

He lit the cigarette and went on. 'Now, think of cards as a Platonic dialogue,' he said. 'You are dealt a completely random hand. You study it thoughtfully and make a proposition. Your opponent with his own cards contradicts it. You then seek to show the inadequacy of his contradiction. You are both drawn into the problem and, when one of you eventually produces cards that are irrefutable, he wins. You have arrived at a temporary solution. Each hand is a staging post on the road to further inquiries.'

'Well, I think we should abandon further inquiries straight away. They are expensive.'

'A financier has sometimes to go on enduring losses because he knows he will profit in the end.'

'And you are certain we will win eventually?'

'In an ideal world.'

'In an ideal world, sticking to a wrong idea is pig-headedness.'

'There are many gamblers who are not content until they have lost. You never know when you have reached your level of incompetence until you have tried. Besides, if I died with money in the bank I would consider myself a failure.'

'But it's not your money.'

'True,' he said, laughing, 'but you are trying to reconcile predestination and human freedom. Learning is recollection. I remember that we shall win. Believe me. All knowledge is recollection. Plato.'

That night we won back almost as much as I had lost during the whole of the previous week.

'You see,' Papantonis said. We were sitting at a blue-painted table on the edge of the road by the town beach. The Americans were with us. We were to eat together. I was pleasantly tired from the idle, day-long ecstasy of the beach and the drowsing sea, and my hair was stiff with salt.

'There is a passage in the *Phaedo*,' Papantonis began saying while reaching for an olive, 'in which Socrates maintains that to do philosophy is to rehearse for death, and so is playing cards.'

He had no chance to explain this idea because both of us followed the direction of the Americans' eyes, and the subject dropped.

Someone said, 'My God. Will you look at that?'

A naked woman was walking towards the town out of the sea. She was not 19, but on a grand scale and extremely statuesque.

While she was still some way off the beach, with the water round her thighs, she encountered coral or sharp stones and began to stagger in an undignified way from side to side, sometimes doubled up and sometimes leaning back.

But when she reached the fine shingle of the beach she walked upright, leisurely, enjoying the attention, resplendent. And, when she was only ankle deep, she paused. There was a hush. In a loud voice she declaimed two lines of ancient Greek poetry.

There was a smattering of applause. Then she stepped forward out of the sea and an attendant handed her a short white beach-robe, which she put on, and gold sandals.

'It's Marjorie Watson,' one of the Americans said. 'She was put off a cruise ship we were in last year because she caused so much trouble.'

Papantonis was laughing. Tears of laughter ran down into his beard.

'I think you mean Phryne,' he said, 'the first female nude.'

'Yes. But what did she recite?' I asked him.

'It was Sappho. It has been translated as: Love has unbound my limbs and set me shaking. A monster bitter-sweet and my unmaking.'

But Marjorie Watson was now on her way past.

Recognizing the Americans, she stopped at our table. At close quarters she was certainly on a magnificent scale, an over-life-size sculpture, dripping from the sea, exhilarated by the success of her performance.

She paid no attention to Papantonis, who was wiping his

eyes with a handkerchief. When I was introduced to her she said 'Darling!' and smiled at me with such radiance that I was almost knocked over.

Then, swaying, and followed by her attendant, she continued on up the slope in the direction of the only good hotel.

★

All that night we played cards against the Americans.

'Mathematical order,' Papantonis said, 'as in cards, replaces disorder throughout the universe.'

I thought he looked fulfilled and supremely happy. Towards midnight he smiled at me and said, 'Short the way, but pitiless the need to walk it.'

'What?'

'Alcman. Dorian about 620 B.C. Good, isn't it?'

'But what was he writing about?'

'Night. Sleep. In this case the path to death.'

Towards dawn, Papantonis and I were at last on the point of becoming rich. He picked up his last hand, and opened with two spades. I bid four spades. When I laid my cards down it became apparent that, with five more tricks to make, all the cards on the table were winners and Papantonis would have no difficulty in achieving a grand slam. He had been waiting for divinely ordered completeness all his life, and here it was. It was, after all, simple. From Revelations. A revelation. He won trick after trick.

Then he led the seven of clubs and boxed himself into the wrong suit. He had kept no spade back with which to get across, and we would go down.

Unforgivably, forgetting myself entirely, I jumped to my feet and shouted at him. He looked at me, smiling, and I pushed him so that he fell off his chair. He lay awkwardly on the floor for a few moments, making a strange noise which sounded very much like laughter. And, when we turned him onto his back, he was dead.

No relations came to his funeral but almost everyone on the

island seemed to know him.

I followed his blackened face on its bier in the pitiless sun. At the head of a cortège, he was carried up the long series of shallow steps to his monastery. Long ago its interior had been marred by fire, and the halos of saints in its wall-paintings were turned black.

Much was said and sung about the seven churches of Asia, and the seven stars, while I thought about the seven of clubs.

Afterwards I saw blackness in the sun. No sanctuary existed for my guilt and grief. Papantonis' heart had burst. I paid the Americans their winnings, and they saw no point in saying I had touched him.

The old blind woman who sold lottery tickets in the square told me that Papantonis had been giving her money, and I went on doing so on his behalf.

11

In a trance of melancholy, I boarded the boat. I was returning to Paris. The island, when about to disappear from sight, lay like the white bones of a carcass beyond the dazzling bay. I turned away from it.

Ten minutes later a launch caught up with us and, smashing up and down on the water, circled us and then came alongside with a flourish. In it were two policemen and, standing in the bows like a figurehead, Marjorie Watson. Her considerable hair was stretched back in the spray.

Our engines reduced to dead slow. One of the policemen, wearing dark glasses, called out my name and made a formal request in Greek for me to disembark. When I went to the lower deck with my bag and jumped across into the bucking launch, Marjorie Watson looked at me with joy.

'You have to come back, darling,' she said in English. 'More questions about Papantonis.'

'We are all products of our own catastrophes.'

'And of our good fortune,' she added with exaggerated kindness. 'Nothing to worry about.'

The Eumenides means the kindly ones, I thought, as the island grew in size again and the familiar buildings of Papantonis, which an hour earlier I had supposed I was abandoning forever, loomed large.

Crates from an impounded merchant ship were being unloaded in the harbour.

When Marjorie and I walked into the town it was as though she made a chorus of old men catalogue her splendours in the Greek drama. Her money and glamour howled in the streets. There was a stench of them across the island.

'My condition is marginal,' I said. 'I feel as if I had arranged to meet Papantonis for cards but come to the wrong place.'

'At the wrong time,' she added, opening a door. 'This is your room.' She smiled at me blindingly with her heavily made-up eyes.

It was a sombre room with a mirror in it.

'I almost got away,' I said.

'Yes, but what happened was only a prelude to much else.'

'Was it?'

'Yes.'

'To me it is more like a daydream than a tragedy,' I said. 'I am disorientated. I feel I am in this place but not of it, and have lost myself.'

There was a long pause. In the gloom her profile and full-face suggested different characters, one anarchic, one serene.

She was a woman who evidently found it difficult to keep her clothes on.

'The temples have fallen but the gods survive,' she said.

★

The ancient Greeks believed that one of the first signs of civilisation was forethought. I made no effort to think ahead. Marjorie Watson looked after me with passionate intensity, and for weeks I remained in the semi-darkness indoors. Eventually it became winter, and still no one questioned me about the death of Papantonis.

Marjorie said, 'I wear my nakedness like a robe. It gives me pleasure to give pleasure.' I had no opinions either way. In fact, it embarrassed me that she had conceived a passion for me which I had done nothing to promote, and I felt little sympathy for her.

When she talked, it was in a fragmentary way. 'My husband, like Heracles, went off to sack a conglomerate,' she said.

She wore her hair rolled up on top of her head, which made her appear even more enormously tall. When she visited me she seemed to bring the lapis sea into the room with her.

I felt as a boy feels when being shielded by his mother against the dangers of the outside world, or like an adolescent she protects from the wiles of dangerous women.

In the room some classical fragments lay about in the gloom: a carved foot in a sandal, coloured glass, the shaft of a column, tacked-up postcards of classical sites. Against them her nudity was creamy, like the art of the museums.

I never asked her anything. 'Since you ask,' she said, 'I have spent a fortune looking for spiritual fulfilment. I considered setting up a sect of my own based on the Aztecs. Now I see that I was misguided.'

She took to wearing what she said was ancient Greek scent, and her neck smelled of warm incense. She became the priestess of the oracle, and her painted eyes blazed with prophetic vision. Like a mannequin, she put on ancient Greek robes. She clambered with difficulty onto the table. 'Look at this,' she said, 'and this. You recognize them?' They were poses from Greek vases.

'I am doing them in public,' she said. 'Greek tragedy began in ritual performance. It contains the seeds of almost everything. I have had an insight.'

As time passed, her jewellery became ever more dazzling. She ripened towards an apotheosis like that of the famous pre-war department store on which her fortune was founded.

She composed, and played on flutes and small antique cymbals, a curious music of her own, full of odd modal and diatonic inconsistencies, which she thought approximated to the music of ancient Greece. Her natural radiance became almost blinding. With gold on her arms and breasts, she stood with extreme gestures, breathing incense and smoke, a giantess in enormous robes.

She had understood that what she truly wanted was to become a goddess.

'First,' she said, 'we must get married. I have sent to Voukourestiou Street, in Athens, for the licence.'

'I will grow to hate you.'

'I am mad for myth.'

The town hall on the square at the top of the town had an enamel crest on the front with, on either side of it, flags in brackets, as on a legation. The mayor's office was like a railway booking-hall. There was a stopped clock, an outsize desk, wooden racks and pigeonholes for mail, an old Greek Airlines poster on the wall.

We signed our names. The mayor, who was a witness, very much wanted Marjorie to fund a festival of Greek ritual in the summer, which she had promised to do. He had a wall eye and a heavy moustache, and shook hands with us most enthusiastically after the ceremony.

When we emerged, the sun tried to damage me as it had done before. It was late May. The sleeping town was already dusty, exhausted. Tamarisks did their worst. Papantonis was nowhere to be seen.

I would have asked him about Orestes. 'You don't see them. You don't. But I see them. They are hunting me down. I must move on.'

'Our wedding was not the beginning of something but the end,' Marjorie said that night. 'You know that, don't you?'

And, shortly afterwards, I succeeded in leaving the island for good.

12

When I got back to Paris, Alain, my activist cousin at Nanterre, was in prison. He had been arrested together with other students who had succeeded in setting fire to the Bourse in May. De Gaulle, expecting revolution, had disappeared and turned out to be at Baden-Baden, talking to the army. I was too late for the riots, and my father had still not completed his equation. It was my belief that his life-long addiction to sleeping tablets had altered the chemistry of his brain and was to blame for his foul temper. The big furniture in his rooms looked like traps.

'That's your post-graduate year wasted,' he said. 'What on earth have you been doing?'

'I was in Greece.'

'Yes, but what doing?'

'First I think and then I draw my think,' I said.

'Are you mad?'

'The sane are madder than you suppose, and the mad saner.'

'I am much too tired for this.' He cracked his fingers irritably. 'Now that you are an architect, suppose you build something?'

'Haussmann pulled down 27,000 houses in Paris between 1853 and 1869.'

'So what will you do?'

'I am going to Naples to open an architects' office there.'

He stood up and walked round me in a circle, seeming to hump the back of his neck in an effort to overcome his stammer.

'Really?' he said. 'F-flies and slums. Revolting. I suppose you will need some m-money.'

It was extremely hot and crowded on the train. I sat on the floor of a third-class carriage, which was like an oven, because my money had not yet come through.

Naples, between action and repose, had chosen to do nothing. Monuments to conquerors and benefactors were parked in the sun, and public buildings, faced with heroic mosaics, were closed for a saint's day. A bride in a white dress and veil crossed the pavé on the arm of her husband on their way to a bar. A boy with a cardboard suitcase on his back ran down a bank of shingle. An undertaker walked purposefully past carrying a gigantic wreath. Cranes by the harbour were stationary.

I took a room next to a photographer's shop with an awning over it. Swifts screamed. A man on a bench opposite was reading a newspaper which turned out to be a musical score.

The owner of the photographer's shop was half Japanese. His name was Y. Y. Laing. He spoke Italian with a Neapolitan accent, in a low voice as if afraid of being overhead.

'I came here,' he said, smiling and frowning simultaneously in a friendly gap-toothed way, 'because Vesuvius reminds me of Mount Fuji. What about you?'

'I feel sober only when I'm drunk.'

'In Naples the conversation of drunks is carried on mostly with the shoulders. The less drunk use their hands. The least drunk make points with the eyes or nose alone.'

Behind his shop was a ramshackle studio in which he specialized in group photographs of ecclesiastical subjects and the poor, mostly votive set-pieces and studies for funerals.

'But how do the poor pay?' I asked.

'They mostly pay eventually. I charge very little, and they almost always pay in the end as a matter of honour. Most charges connected with illness and death in Naples are regarded as a legitimate expense, including my photographs of the dead and dying. The funerals of destitute people are often grandiloquent. It is a question of appearances. Many of the poor live packed tightly into rooms with no water or electricity in houses that have magnificent façades, and bankrupts are buried in gilt coffins.'

The equipment in his studio was old. Some of his cameras still took glass negatives.

'I bought them years ago with the shop and they were old then,' he said, 'but there is every reason to go on using them.'

'Why?'

'You have never lived here so you will not understand.'

'There is hardly any light in here,' I said, looking at the cracked and yellowing glass roof of his studio. It was a blazing day outside. 'I should re-design the roof for you. And your architectural props stand on carpet.'

'True,' he said. 'That is the point of them. There is much you don't yet know about Naples. But now I have the brigadiere in charge of the local carabinieri calling to tell me about the death of his mother. Even carabinieri have mothers apparently.'

Next day was a feast day and it was hotter still. The city wore an aluminium halo. Y. Y. Laing failed to appear in the osteria at which we had arranged to meet, nor was he in his shop or studio. But he was in his place at the osteria two days later.

'Yesterday was a martyr's feast day, you understand,' he said, waving me to a seat, 'and it is considered by many to be perfectly reasonable to spend martyrs' days in a stupor or semi-conscious. In Naples it is practically a way of life to make allowances for the supernatural. Besides, to believe otherwise is bad luck, and in Naples luck is paramount.'

'You were going to explain about your photographs.'

'Was I? You don't even know yet how to eat macaroni in the approved manner with your hands.'

'No.'

'Or the appropriate way in which to eat spaghetti.'

'No.'

He indicated, with a slight flick of his head, a diner seated behind him. 'Watch closely. It is much more difficult than it looks.'

'What else?'

'Everything is to do with Catholicism. Not only churches. Visit a religious supplies shop. Immerse yourself in it. Buy medals and trinkets, those little tin limbs, feet, ears and eyes. For medals, start with San Rocco. Look at dead saints. Try to see liquefactions. In Naples, Catholicism in its most exaggerated form has metamorphosed virtually into a form of paganism. It is part of life in the same way that Marsala is mixed with the yolk of eggs.'

He took off his hat and wiped his head with a handkerchief.

'And most of all,' he went on, 'you should look at the ex-votos in the dark corners of chapels. Primitive paintings on board. Mostly 19th-century, cack-handed but often beautiful in their way. They use bright colours, red, yellow, blue, representing tragedies. Usually they show the sufferer, the dying person, in bed, with above them – apparently in the room – a hovering vision of Christ on the cross, Mary and the Christ child, a pietà or Christ carrying the cross.'

'Intercessions by prayer?'

'Certainly they are intercessions, in a passionate and melodramatic form. Votive pictures bring onto the stage entire dramatic spectacles in which God himself, the Virgin Mary, saints, martyrs and angels all make their appearances in person. They visit the torments of the living, the sufferings of the dying, as they might visit the more entertaining categories of hell. They plead, entreat and implore God to grant forgiveness and put an end to suffering.'

'You are moved by it.'

'Of course. Who would not be? They even pray for a respite. The people weep and kiss the ground. "Heal me that I may behold Thee." Their tears flow upwards to heaven.'

'Not something you can show in a photograph.'

'I can do it if necessary by photographing the beatific vision in some other form and placing it over the ill person by making use of a double negative.'

'You mean, photograph effigies and sculptures and superimpose them?'

'Certainly. And the votive paintings are a marvellous source because they frequently depict the accident that has caused the trouble in the first place. Their awkward subjects are boundless. Run over by a cart. Fallen from a balcony. Gored by a bull. Drowned. Shot in battle. Bitten by a dog. Trapped in a burning building. A mistake on the operating table.'

'And all this is the reason that you photograph priests?'

'They crawl to me. I photograph them kneeling. In my

pictures they contemplate crucifixes held up before their eyes. They can maintain expressions of rapture for minutes on end. They love the vanitas and memento mori, and will rivet their attention on a skull or on an open Bible for long periods without blinking.'

'I can see why,' I said.

'Sometimes they beat their breasts with rocks.'

'But the poor just stare at the camera.'

He smiled. 'You are very persistent. Have you ever considered silence?'

He paused while an old man came up to our table and tried to sell us printed fortunes. A goat standing in a small cart was towed past by a man on a bicycle. A girl in a dress with shoulder pads came out of a shop which sold tripe. When the old man had gone away, Y. Y. Laing said, 'If you must know, I think my photographs have much to do with silence.'

I waited quietly and after another long pause he said, 'Naples is a place of din. Not only the traffic. People here speak in raised voices, shout across the street, argue, have hysterics, hurl abuse, yell accusations, scream greetings. They are full of bawdy chattering. But then there is also silence, the silence of those to whom as a punishment nothing is said for years and who are silent in return. The silence of churches and of the preserved corpses of saints. That is the same silence. I try to talk quietly and often I would prefer not to speak at all. Of course, my photographs are completely silent.'

He looked at me, wondering whether it was worth his while to go on. At last he did.

'When the poor come into my studio, they are partly cowed by it and by the apparatus. I do not attempt to put them at their ease. In fact, I believe that sitters should be ill at ease. In the best photographs they usually are. Their hubbub is left outside. It is left outside in the place where they eat refuse and live crammed together, their lives wrecked by infection, prostitution, drugs, corruption, perversion, crime, and the most terrible misapprehensions with the camorrista which can often lead to life-long victimization. They live in terror of being misunderstood, and about their only recreation is in public places, in the street, in the high spirits and uproar of public festivals. Many of them are half starved. They live by trying to sell cigarette butts and offal thrown away by osterias like this one. Sex is their opera.'

A fly landed on his face and started towards his eye, which was watering, but he disregarded it.

'When such people enter my studio they are often silent. They keep their distance from the camera. They look with curiosity at my fairground props, the background with a grand salon painted on it, a screen depicting waves at the edge of the sea, fragments of plaster ruins, dilapidated upholstery.

'I arrange sitters formally in rows, knowing that the camera will pay equal attention to small things and large, to the crease in a drape and the crease in a face, to the base of a column standing on a piece of carpet. They are wearing their best clothes and often borrowed shoes. Sometimes they have bare feet. Almost all sitters have blemishes of one form or another, and some have many. They are marks of suffering of which they are proud. The camera is extremely observant of the blemish.

'If people want a big print I have to use a big camera. When the group is arranged and the camera is aimed, I take a sheet of glass and perform what must seem to them a kind of conjuring trick or miracle. Onto the plate I pour collodion, which contains potassium oxide. As soon as it is evenly coated, I dip it quickly in silver nitrate and place it in the dark slide. It has to be exposed immediately, before the ether evaporates from the collodion, or the plate will become insensitive. Because of the low light in the studio the exposure has to be very long. And during this long exposure, which is sometimes over a minute, something very odd happens. Something that to me is still in a way religious.'

'To do with time'.

'In a way.'

'And to do with you?'

'No. It has nothing to do with me. I do no more than point the camera.'

'So what is the extraordinary thing that the camera does?'
'It shows the world exactly as it isn't.'
'As it is, surely.'
'No. It doesn't see the world as we see it, for one very good reason.'
'And what is that?'
'The answer is simple. It refuses to discriminate. The camera is a machine which obviously has no way of knowing what is important and what isn't, so it gives everything equal emphasis, which is not at all like life, and even less like art. But that is still not it, not quite.'

I waited for him to go on. It seemed extraordinary to me that a process with which he was so familiar still struck him as such a mystery.

He said, 'After the exposure there has to be another burst of violent activity. I hurry about and develop the plate as quickly as I can in protosulphate of iron, and fix it using potassium cyanide. Often sweat and insects make blots and streaks on the uneven coating, and I get dizzy from the fumes.'

'So there is haste and messiness, you mean, both before and after the long stillness of the exposure?'

'Messiness, yes. I like the messiness. I like blots. They give immediacy, and the sitters do not seem to mind them.'

'But that's not it?'
'No. Not quite.'
'What then?'
'Their gaze.'
'The gaze of the sitters?'
'Yes. During the long exposure the sitters must not move, must not blink, almost must not breathe, and they will remain motionless in the photograph ever afterwards. I am tempted to say they are pinned so that, with absolute objectivity, the camera can look into their very identity. If I were religious, I would say into their souls. At any rate, into the dark. They look into the camera and the camera looks into them. The wet-plate process has a very high contrast and it is completely merciless. The sit-

ters' unnatural and self-conscious stillness in the present is made by the photograph to become incorruptible, to last more or less forever.'

'Until they are anonymous?'

'Yes, and always in the present,' said Y. Y. Laing, brushing away the fly. 'Always exactly in the present. So I fear that, in the end, the poor in my photographs are more alive when they are dead.'

13

When my money came through I erected a site-hut on waste ground behind Y. Y. Laing's studio and set to work. Opposite the studio, wedged into the space where two roads forked, there was a corner bar, narrow as a slim slice of tart.

After I had laboured for two years without letting up, I began to see what might be possible. I took on three assistants and began submitting plans to competitions for city projects.

The oldest and most dignified of my new assistants was Giorgio Ippolito, a tall and cadaverous man who was obsessed with the Golden Mean.

He was never in any hurry and was always courteous. Whenever he answered the telephone he asked sedately, *'Con qui parlo?'*

It was a period which lacked innovation in public planning, and I soon found that theoretical ideas which I had first sketched out as an architectural student now had practical applications. My mind ran to several projects at once, and I experienced a gratifying appetite of the sort which has come over me from time to time, as it had when I discovered Krzysztof Cviic's film.

Giorgio kept a sceptical eye on me.

'Vide papier que la blancheur defend,' he said at the beginning, but I had started to find that blank paper produced an almost erotic effect on me, with its invitation to make something out of nothing.

What was more, I felt in touch with my younger self, as though my early sketches and drawings were a form of communication between us as tangible as letters. I could imagine the younger self spying on me as I was now, looking in at the window of the site-hut drawing office, amazed to see what I had become as he peered over my shoulder at his old evolving plans.

'Here is what I want to do,' I said one day to Y. Y. Laing, who always listened with attention. 'Despite all the thought, I want to have an element of chance in my buildings, the same chance as in painting and poetry when things seem to come together of their own accord. I want my ideas to have amplitude, boldness, even lavishness. I want them to embody contradictions, which are natural and essential. I want them to originate in the street, from among the same poor you are always photographing. The most extraordinary things are the most everyday.'

'Yes. But how to draw them?'

'Drawing them presents few problems. They must be logical, stripped, pure, clear, free of compromises, witty, consoling. They must effortlessly transcend every technical difficulty and remain uncorrupted by ego. Even out of everyday life, which is egotistical and confused, it must occasionally be possible to construct work which is eloquent and serene. You do it.'

Y. Y. Laing looked doubtful. 'So you are intending to build for the poor?' he said.

'Of course. What better project? It was you who first described to me their atrocious conditions. Instead of living in windowless rooms, choked by dust, they will be lifted by my schemes into light and air. My plans are for much more than just social housing with balconies, sea air and palm-shaded gardens. Giorgio Ippolito will make sure that every design is related to the beautiful proportions of his beloved Golden Mean. All will be as clean and compact as the living accommodation in a perfectly planned ship.'

'They will not thank you for it, and as things stand,' Y. Y. Laing said, 'every available space is crammed. Louse-ridden slums and tenement blocks stretch in a fiery haze from here to Castellamare.'

But Pompeo, in the wedge-shaped bar across the road, was a

strong supporter of my schemes.

'By the Holy Virgin and the Sacred Heart, what drawings!' he said. 'I never saw a Christian soul make better drawings. Air-conditioning? By God's grace let the scheme be built. Christ's providence will see it built.'

He owned a dachshund which had put its back out trying to beg, and dragged itself around on rear wheels. Pompeo tried his best to communicate his excitement and anticipation to the dog. If there was no one else in, he would go on about the drawings to the dachshund, it being a captive audience. The dog hated him.

'Thanks be to God for such an architect, eh? Long live the architect!' he would say. 'His scheme, just let them try and stop it. Bastards!'

Within six months, my practice had twice won architectural competitions with large-scale innovative designs for public housing. The judges praised the beauty of our plans and I was invited to tender proposals for another even larger scheme, the re-building of the Suore Benedittine di Montevergine, a city hospital for the poor, for derelicts and old people, together with an associated orphanage.

With Giorgio's help, I negotiated to obtain an altered site which would enable me to turn the hospital round and re-align it above the bay, so as to catch light and sea air, on rising ground, clear of pollution.

All day and night I thought of nothing but this building and of what I could bring to it. My imagination raced.

I began to envisage it in terms of music, full of repeating phrases, internal harmonies and great silences which were to be the airy intervals and interludes within its mass. The shade and space between its elements were to be as important and health-giving as the structures themselves, because it is when people are ill that they most need space and room to breathe.

At last I had a chance to build something that could give sufferers back their health and sanity. I thought in terms of a resplendent purity, resplendent geometry, and of buildings which could transform every aspect of life. I would design each detail of them down to hospital clothing and lettering, making use of austere forms. I would use porous materials to absorb sound and make for quietness. I would design fittings that folded away to make spaces larger, always with reference to the reach and dimensions of the human body. And on a cleared site, uncluttered, I would lay out buildings on a humane scale, with forms like music which begins before it is heard and continues when it is out of earshot.

As Giorgio often said, 'All freedoms belong to architecture except that of not being clear.'

I began to see inspiration all around me, in the shapes of pasta, in the shapes of coffee machines, in the shapes of the paper hats worn by house-painters.

All the time I drew, devising new solutions for each function of the hospital. Something was running riot in my head. I was mad for design. Given the opportunity, I would have designed beds, wheelchairs, surgical instruments, hypodermic syringes. Even stationery, fonts, and the way people write and speak.

I made Giorgio flap sheets with me to analyse their billowing surfaces. I teased him by pointing out that you could spend your whole life fiddling around with proportions and still not sing. When occasionally I sat to eat, I put my eye down to the table to find how one glass masked another, to see the gaps between bottles and dishes, imagining them as buildings against blue sky. I liked working with engineers. With them I improvised novel solutions. I scribbled, often without looking at the page, in the hope that random lines would turn up chance ideas, providing leaps and surprises I could never expect to arrive at by thinking. My designs must be fluid. I returned often in my memory to Lipstick Matabele's Morandi, to Boccioni, and to Brancusi's sculpture studio in Paris. And always I thought how beautifully light pours over buildings far away.

I took on four more draughtsmen, the youngest of whom was Fausto Bassi, and worked with indefatigable enthusiasm at all hours. I worked in the osteria and in bars, and I worked in my head when I was walking in the street. I worked in my sleep, dreaming of beyond what is possible and already known.

'I feel very ignorant about all this,' I confessed one day to Giorgio, to which he replied, 'Ignorance is essential. If we knew how difficult they are, we would not attempt half the things we do.'

And all the time, like a man who cranes round in an attempt not to lose sight of his own shadow, I remained in touch with my previous self, so easily do we become estranged from our previous selves when the circumstances of our lives alter.

★

Giorgio Ippolito and I went from Naples, through the suburbs and Battipaglia, from dust, haze and scorched oleanders to the tortoise-ridden rubble and ant-infested overgrown ruins of the great classical site of Paestum. Giorgio had his chess set with him.

'I have tried the temples many times,' he said, 'and they are always the same. That is the point of them.'

'I suppose you resent your country's architecture invariably belonging to the past. The dead hand. Museums like mausoleums, and visitors only looking at archaeological sites. At anything worn out by the sun, like us.'

'It's not that,' he said.

It was the hottest time of day at the hottest time of year when we arrived at Paestum, and, apart from an American woman with a red parasol, there was nobody else there. The three temples, their honey-coloured stone catching the light among parched vegetation, with the occasional cypress, stone pine or pomegranate tree, occupied their flat plain. There were green and blue lizards on the stones and, inland, in the distance, the blue angular hills that are part of the Cilento massif.

Giorgio said nothing as we walked down the ancient central strada, paved with large, hot lapides and lacking shade. I wondered what was preoccupying him, the modern architect. When we reached the Temple of Poseidon, he sat down in the shade of a stone pine and set up his chessboard. He and I sat either side of a flat block of stone. We must have looked like the tiny figures put into an 18th-century print to suggest scale.

'Chess is in two dimensions,' he said, 'and the game is limited by rules, precise, definite and without distractions. Nothing is miscellaneous or irrelevant. Eight rows across, eight vertically, 64 squares. A perfect symmetry.'

He hesitated before making a simple opening. I made the appropriate response and, unhurriedly, we began to play.

After a quarter of an hour I said, 'I thought you were going to tell me about the architecture.'

'We are not adrift in formlessness and confusion,' he replied, 'but established in a dimension. Most people are trapped in the present.'

'You are going to tell me that what most pleases the eye is unity in diversity.'

'I wasn't, but I think that is true.'

'That is rational but, in architecture, isn't there something else, something more?'

'How do you mean?'

'Cannot architecture be suggestion rather than statement in some way, like a waking dream?'

'½ ($\sqrt{5} \pm 1$).'

'Exactly,' I said. 'You can provide the rational and I will do my best to come up with the dream.'

I looked over his head at the solemn beauty of the Doric columns, at their progress and regular repetitions, in which nothing was wasted, nothing extraneous. The temples were beautiful from a distance and superb close-to. Structures for time, uncluttered, continuous, replete.

I said, 'You mean the past has become the present? The new forever new?'

'No.'

'What then? The Greeks had relatively little past, and the past is mostly ours? Or is it your obsession with proportion again?'

'Light and shadow. The black and white chess pieces, the alternating squares of the board. The virtue of the columns is that they both conceal and expose. Every action or inaction, every move, has its consequences.'

He was smiling now. 'You surely don't need a lesson on entasis and architraves.'

'I would not mind.'

'Part of the reason that the columns behind me gather and hold light so beautifully is that they each have 24 rather than the usual 20 flutes. The Greeks made their humanity evident within the context of order.'

He glanced down at the chessboard and made his riposte at once, as if needing no time to recognize my strategy. I suspected him of owning a book of chess problems. In fact, he seemed to expect my secret purposes, but this did not trouble me because I was beginning to enjoy myself. It was pleasant in the shade. Nothing in the whole landscape moved except for the red parasol of the distant American woman as she picked her way among the rubble.

'Go on about time,' I said.

'Which time? You seem to want to lose yourself in pleasant generalities brought on by the satisfying monotony of the columns and their perspectives. On the chessboard you think things over at a little distance, and the regular progression of the columns has a view beyond them to the distant hills, where they grow vines. Dimension does not depend on unpredictability. Because it is orderly, it can also be ample, effulgent, existing in deep time, and have vistas.'

'Viewing the present as a future memory, you mean?'

Giorgio looked at me as if he thought I would do better not to speak, but I went on regardless.

'This place answers all my cravings,' I said. 'All the cravings I have ever felt in architecture for form, volume, weight, mass, interval, rhythm, proportion, harmony, stasis and movement.'

'The chessboard within yourself.'

'No. Not tricks and stratagems of attack and defence, not

guessing and crossing, but a sense of structure in uninterrupted time.'

After a pause, Giorgio said, 'Uninterrupted time? For 800 years nothing interrupted these temples except water-buffalos and crows.'

He moved a pawn. 'The entire plain became a malarial swamp.'

I tried to imagine the ruins interrupted only by marsh and the persistent grey-green multiplication of reeds while history came and went.

'And when were the ruins rediscovered?'

'They were permanently interrupted in 1752.'

'In time for Piranesi?' I said.

'It was his last job.'

I looked at the clear vista, at the blue of the distant mountains between the columns. I liked seeing through buildings from one end to the other. Admitting maximum light, with economy of means, I must design the same. For the same air and light.

'I wish Corot had come here,' I said, 'and painted it simply, from a distance, across the plain.'

'With large dimensions of time.'

'Yes. With large dimensions of time, and on a particular day.'

'This particular day.'

I was looking up at the mighty west gable of the temple of Poseidon, and at that moment I saw it crack. A jagged line appeared suddenly and made its way from the trabeation through the triglyphs and fronton to near the apex of the pediment, letting through a sliver of distant sky.

'Buildings which have endured,' Giorgio was saying, with his back to this, unaware, 'are beautiful because they are complete in their present and in ours.'

White-faced, I said hoarsely, 'It just cracked.'

'Doesn't matter,' he replied. 'Your move.'

14

'Who is that?' I asked Y. Y. Laing when he showed me some recent photographs and asked my opinion of them.

'The cousin from Venice.'

'He looks familiar,' I said.

It was a photograph of a funeral group. In the middle was the body of a dead baby propped up in a white dress and surrounded by lilies, a small cross in her raised hand. Her parents, grandparents, brothers and sisters were seated on either side or standing behind her, but at the right-hand end of the back row was a man who appeared conspicuously different from the rest. He was handsome, elderly, with thin hair combed back and an air of patrician aloofness.

'I see you do not know about cousins from Venice,' said Y. Y. Laing. 'There is one at most Neapolitan weddings and funerals. By the poor they are considered practically indispensible. They lend prestige and a distinct hint that the family has distinguished connections. They say almost nothing, but when they do speak it is always with a cultivated accent. They are deliberately unapproachable and remain distant.'

He smiled and scowled simultaneously as he looked down at the photograph. 'Yes. This is a particularly good example,' he said. 'They are almost always fakes.'

'Not relations at all?'

'No. There are a number of older men with a distinguished appearance and rudimentary acting ability who are professional cousins from Venice or sometimes from Florence. They can be hired. It provides employment and they are seldom found out because everyone colludes.'

'I think I have seen this one before.'

'It's more than likely. I certainly have. The trouble is, I have photographed them so often that by now they all look alike to me. More or less.'

'It is a pity about the girl who moved,' I said, pointing to a blurred figure near the front.

'Yes. She has done that since she was a child. Every time I photograph the Bassi family she comes out as a blur. To her, sitting still is an impossibility. She has ruined countless photographs of mine. It used to annoy me but now I just accept it, and the family never seems to mind. In fact it has become something of a joke. In some ways the blur is exactly like her.'

'How do you mean?'

'She is always in motion. She is obsessed with speed. I have no idea what she was christened but she is known to everyone as Velocità.'

Shortly after this I was on my way to a site meeting with Giorgio when I was almost knocked down by a girl on a Vespa. She looked 13 and was at full speed. She was laughing.

'That was Fausto Bassi's sister,' Giorgio said. 'She is called Velocità. If you can, it is safest to keep clear of her. Several of the women in the Bassi family have killed themselves.'

Fortunately, Giorgio was a reliable and persistent negotiator who knew everybody and understood how the contorted planning system worked. As the hospital project advanced, there were visits made by Fausto Bassi to the bureaus of city officials to discuss site-lines and drainage. Mercenary dealings connected with contracts and the Neapolitan Civil Engineer's department I left entirely to Giorgio, and he had the tact not to trouble me with them.

The most he would say in his beautiful Italian was, 'He was happy to accept our alms with one eye closed and the other dry.'

Towards the end of June he had a visit from Fausto Bassi's elder brother, Umberto, who said that he was on excellent terms with the brother-in-law of the mayor, who happened to have a reinforced concrete business. I explained that I was not using reinforced concrete.

'There is bound to be plenty of this kind of thing,' Y. Y. Laing said when I told him about it, 'especially with a project as large as your hospital. In Naples it is necessary to keep your nerve.

Sometimes faults and vices are the corollary of virtues.'

*

A year later I took a train down the coast to Castellabate.
Santa Maria di Castellabate is an ancient port bunged up with burning sand. Scorched, narrow streets draped with washing. Boats tied up beside a row of Roman arches. A brightly painted effigy of Santa Maria della Mare overlooking the beach. Old people, burned black, in the windows of derelict houses. Ants. Newspapers. Litter. Fans. Card-players. A beach-bar infested with brown children. The street-cry of a man selling vegetables from the back of a lorry. A cat shot with a pistol. A crab tormented by a dog. Passages. Radios. Steps. Drains. Bells. Motorbikes. Laughter. Shutters. Bougainvillaea. Fat palm trees in sand. Cactuses with toes. Women laying tables in gloomy rooms. The smells of fish. Death notices pasted up on peeling walls.

The town becomes a richer ochre as the sun goes down, and the bird in a cage on a window-ledge by the beach sings more loudly. When the red sun touches the horizon the bird abruptly stops singing and the sea turns to milk.

. In the evening I boarded the exhausted cream-painted bus, with 'Venus' written on the side, and went up the mountain behind the town to a restaurant which Giorgio had shown me soon after I first arrived in Naples.

That day with Giorgio, I had drawn on a paper napkin a suggested scheme for a system of movable box hedges for the restaurant terrace. The watered box had grown well, and I now sat in a pleasant green room on the terrace which overlooked the mountainside and the sea.

Behind me was the gatto-ridden, bell-ridden, rotting mountain-top town, a place of stone passages and steps, arches, belfries, derelict altarpieces and reliquaries, its church full of portraits of 18th-century canons in red vestments, each keeping his place in the missal of the afterlife with a worldly white finger. Some chattering infant-school children, cleaned up for a church festival, the girls in laundered dresses and holding hands, went past on their way to the piazza.

I pretended indifference to myself, but the box design was not what I had come to find. I knew that the place had become the favourite resort of Velocità and the Bassi brothers.

In a few short weeks Velocità's animal vitality, small head and broad shoulders had destroyed my peace of mind. Her youthful magnetism was reckless, indiscriminate and irresistible. I knew that she was devoted to idleness, to the beach and to speed. She made no pretence of being otherwise. But, for all her rapid movement, she was going nowhere. Her high spirits, brown skin and long legs had effortlessly wrecked my self-control. Even now, *soi-même*, I cannot speak adequately of her eyes. They were the most unsettling and destructive eyes I have ever encountered. They were abnormally light-coloured, the colour of water. Not the blue of sea-water but of water in a glass, with blue flecks in it. Their whole irises – not just the pupils – expanded or contracted when her mood changed. Sometimes the two eyes seemed not to be the same colour as one another. One would be almost green and the other almost blue. And yet what was truly alarming was that there was nothing there. Behind them was an absence. The exuberance, lust, amusement, fury or boredom the eyes registered seemed not to have a source. The crazy owner of the personality was not in. Behind the eyes lay no blazing intelligence, no imagination, no passion, no originality, no deep-seated or profound suffering, no melancholy, no insight, just the hollow skull. It was not the least characteristic of those unendurable eyes that they damaged mindlessly, without point and to no purpose.

Part of me dreaded the agonizing restiveness, the irredeemable loss of appetite for anything else that is the result of infatuation. I knew she was not worth the destruction of my work, my ruined concentration or the abandonment of my independence. But I caught my breath when I saw what it was that I had been lying to myself about. I got up and walked to the edge of the cliff.

Far below on the empty road that leads out of the town and

up the mountainside, a solitary vehicle was making its way. From here I could see the whole road, with its hairpin bends and short tunnels. I knew the car very well. It had been built long ago as a racing car with a 15-litre aeroplane engine. Instead of a windscreen it had a semi-circular metal stone-guard. There was a narrow bucket-seat for the driver. Behind it, a bolster tank with two spare tyres secured to it by a strap. There was almost no bodywork. It had no front-wheel brakes. Velocità sat on the car rather than in it, and a thick exhaust-pipe snaked along the side just below her arm. There were heavy chains driving the back axle, and a ramshackle advance-retard lever for the ignition taped to the scuttle. The narrow wheels were kicking up long plumes of white dust.

At the beginning of the summer Velocità had induced a boyfriend, who was a member of the Neapolitan camorristi, to give her this machine as a toy. She kept it in a locked bunker behind the Vesuvio Hotel, but because it could barely pass down the tall, narrow streets of Naples which are the legacy of the original Greek settlement, and because it sometimes caught fire in traffic, it was used by her chiefly on the coast road south to Castellabate. It had to be push-started. In it she was suicidal.

Several times I succeeded in following her part of the way. I watched her drive, in suffocating heat, through the cement-dust suburbs of Naples and then flat out at twice the legal speed-limit past Salerno, round Battipaglia, the ruins at Paestum, and Agropoli. Swerving, cutting in, gesturing, crossing herself when she passed hearses, she thundered down the long straights, past exhausted beach bars, palm trees, oleanders, fig trees. Through dust and haze she took the corners on worn pavé shiny with rubber and oil, past scorched banks and other evidence of fires, past trucks on the railway line and a car in a ravine, until finally she went screaming off the coast road and through the worn-out orchards and dead olive groves with cactuses on broken walls, down into the sun-wrecked streets of Santa Maria di Castellabate.

Now the titanic machine was making its way out of the town

and beginning on the steep ascent to where I stood on the cliff. I could already hear the exhaust. She drove hard up the zig-zag road, past subsidence and unfinished buildings, round hollow olive trees, past umbrella pines, gutters, lines of stones, scorched towers, parched scrubby slopes, drunken trees on dangerous crags, and a burning bank.

As she entered a tunnel I saw her quickly push her goggles up onto her forehead and wrench them down again as she emerged into the light. Her face, arms and legs were black with oil. Flailing chains, valves and the action of the hard springs threw her about. On short straights she leant across and rapidly worked the hand-pump that kept up the fuel pressure. When she was almost unseated by the roughness of the road she clung to the steering-wheel, laughing. The shadow of the big contraption raced beside her on the bank.

I could hear the harsh snarling as the speed of the engine rose and fell. There was a level-crossing behind the town which made the primitive suspension leap, and then Velocità settled to negotiating the long series of tight bends that led up the mountain.

What she could not see was that the bus called Venus, full of the school children I had noticed on their way back from the church festival, was on its dithering return journey, its horn mooing forlornly on the bends.

She and the bus were converging. Neither could see the other and she would certainly not be able to hear the bus's horn over the roar of her own engine.

I knew from my journey up that the bus-driver was a popular, ebullient, bullet-headed, elderly man who wound his wide wheel in a lackadaisical way past his fat stomach, talking and laughing, without paying much attention to the road. The long gearlever, with its broken knob and split rubber housing, he manhandled far back or far forward when necessary while turning round to joke with the friends who stood behind him. Familiar with the more or less empty road all his life, he treated it as his own. He had no qualms about stopping across junctions if that was where passengers wanted to climb up or get down. Sticking his arm out of the window, he was in the habit of laughingly collecting a newspaper from a friend beside the road without troubling to slow down. He was a man entirely happy in his work, with a certain panache born of long familiarity but so relaxed as to have almost no concentration.

He had now pulled up, obstructing the road at a place where Velocità, accelerating round a blind corner, would have no way of avoiding a fatal accident.

And then suddenly there swept over me an immeasurable relief. I knew very well that I would have designed my best buildings expressly for her, and that she would have shown complete indifference to them. I would have sent her my most precious plans and drawings, and she would have forgotten to open the envelopes or thrown them away. I would have lavished all my best ideas on her with not a moment's respite while she continued to ignore me. But we are often numbed by a yearning for things which can never actually exist. At least now I would be able to return to my work untormented. All this I thought in deadly earnest.

But, in the event, Velocità somehow avoided the bus. And her only casualty was me.

15

'So,' said Giorgio Ippolito, who saw it as part of his job to protect me and my work from Velocità, 'you do not like her?'

'No.'

'But that is part of her attraction?'

'The essence of her attraction is that I do not much like her. That is her fascination.'

'She is a child.'

'Yes, but a child-woman.'

These conversations with Giorgio took place in the billiard-room of the Hotel Modena, near my drawing office.

The flies in the bar were terrible, but there was a back room which stayed open all night and was used by those who could not pay for lodgings or were too drunk to find their way home. It had the only billiard table in the neighbourhood and was something of an attraction. They kept an eight-year-old boy there with jug ears who was dressed in a white waistcoat and made to play exhibition matches like a freak. Giorgio and I visited the place about once a month. I pretended to myself that I was still working.

Because Giorgio was yellow, tall and cadaverous, playing against him was like playing billiards with Death.

'And how can you understand a word of what she says to you in Neapolitan dialect?' Giorgio said.

'Almost all of it passes me by.'

'Another way she has of excluding you.'

'I find it one of the more irresistible things about her.'

'You want me to teach it to you?' he asked.

'No.'

'The O becomes a U. It is the pronunciation which makes the line endings of Neapolitan love songs into an *Ooo* instead of the O of Italian. So she does please you although you have nothing in common with her?'

'No, she does not please me,' I said emphatically.

'We may not choose whom we love,' Giorgio said.

Evidently Giorgio had played a great deal of billiards as a young man but he was hampered by his temperament. He would succumb to temptation and, if things were going badly for him, was prone to self-pity. I liked the way the billiard balls crossed the cloth, their collisions and changes of speed, the ellipses they described, their concussions and rebounds. They gave me ideas about geometry and drawing which had to do with architecture. For Giorgio they referred only to the Golden Mean.

'You know she lies to you,' Giorgio said, 'as she does to everyone else.'

'Perhaps, but I think she believes what she is saying.'

'Of course. Like all habitual liars she is sincere while she gives you some totally fictitious account of something she has done. What is worse, she is sure to throw in a few truths and half-truths to keep you happy and to bolster her credibility.'

'You mean that in your opinion she is likely to tell me the same lies she tells everyone else?'

Giorgio looked at me under the yellow gas lamp. The clock on the red wall above the door had stalled at a quarter past midnight. A smart-arse in a straw hat was sitting with a bony-looking prostitute, and the man who worked in the municipal sewerage department – the cause of continuous epidemics – was asleep with his head on the table by the stove.

'The lies with which she flatters you when she is with you are certain to be the very same ones she has told to every other man,' Giorgio said.

'No.'

'If you think she behaves to you any differently you are deluding yourself.'

'Well then, I am deluding myself.'

I saw the room for what it was. It had something sickly about it. In this neighbourhood, churches stood next to brothels as if to prove that faith pardons natural behaviour. But I liked the vivid, flat table, the lilac in a jug on the green counter, the sullen waiter, the dreariness and the bad language. In here everyone had always treated me well, even the police. It was a room in which nothing happened except for occasional altercations but in which it was surely possible to ruin oneself or go mad.

'She is two people,' Giorgio said. 'She is the girl she becomes when she is with you, and the girl you think of when she is not with you.'

On the billiard-table it is extraordinary how persistent bad fortune can be. The butcher, with a dark protuberance on his forehead like a piece of flung liver, came in and sat down opposite the cripple from the button factory. The more crooks and madmen the better, I thought. Giorgio smiled as he totted up easy points, scoring canons with little touches.

'In this room,' he said, 'resides the eternal question: is the whole of life visible to us?'

But the more Giorgio tried to warn me off, the more I thought my passion for Velocità was growing. I felt a fool with her, and was always failing to put myself in the best light because there was nothing about my work, character or appearance that could possibly be of interest to her.

I could not bring myself to accept that the way she flirted with me was no different from the way in which she flirted with most men. I let myself mistake her behaviour and the sentiments she expressed as promises, when all she was doing was leading me around on a string with everyone else. High points for me went unnoticed by her. When I reminded her of our anniversaries she could not remember what I was talking about. The truth was that I loved her for some reason that had nothing whatever to do with her.

Her lying I knew to be several degrees subtler than Giorgio suggested, because more complicated. It was the instinctive fabrication of someone to whom life seemed dull if not lived simultaneously in several different versions. It excited her and she toyed with it endlessly.

When she lied, she told the truth as frequently and in as much detail as possible. This meant that, when she needed not to tell the whole truth, all she had to do was to invent fictions which were inconspicuous perversions of self-evident fact. Then, when it was time for her to lie outright, she covered herself by basing her story, not on the present, but on facts which needed to be remembered by the person she was deluding. This always confused me because, seduced by her glamour, vivacity and apparent sincerity, I would begin to doubt my own version of events, so anxious was I to believe hers.

I understood all this only too well, and I knew Giorgio was right when he said that her secret was to believe in the essential sincerity of falsehood, but still I could do nothing to save myself.

'It might not be so serious,' Giorgio said, 'had you not invited her to Rome.'

'You know nothing about what happened in Rome,' I said, and played a massé shot, holding the cue vertically and driving down so viciously that the struck ball raced round his, sizzling, in an arc, potted the red, touched three cushions and attacked his white from the rear, knocking it deftly into baulk.

What happened in Rome was one more humiliation. I had paid for Velocità to go there, and arranged to meet her at Caffè Greco. Long before the time at which we had agreed to meet I had waited in apprehension at the foot of the Spanish Steps, beneath the window at which it would once have been possible to hear Keats's uncontrollable coughing. There I worked out what I would say to her, and how I would explain to her the depth of my feelings. Then I went into the via Condotti and waited in the caffè among the marble and gilt tables, the tailcoated waiters, the drawings and sculptures and framed letters from Stendhal, Goethe, Berlioz and Grieg and my own foolishly love-struck profile all around me in repeating mirrors.

When she did eventually arrive she was with a laughing and slightly drunk Neapolitan boy her own age.

'At the hospital,' she said, 'they had entertainments. They showed films but it was impossible to concentrate because patients screamed at the screen.'

She had no sooner sat down than she was up again, dancing violently by herself. Everyone else was seated. She waved her arms above her head and threw her legs out disjointedly, her feet turned inwards like a hysteric or a woman suffering an epileptic fit. A whirling universe. A cimbalom played discretely in the background. She lay down on the marble floor and continued dancing frenziedly in a prone position. The waiters watched without giving anything away. No one moved. When she finally stood up and returned to her banquette she looked round the room and said, 'Well, everyone has to go a little crazy occasionally, don't they? It's only natural.'

'We know what you mean,' I said. Then there was a silence broken only by the melancholy voice of the cimbalom.

'So far to come and yet we have nothing to say to one another,' she remarked, shrugging as if she did not hold it against me, but the quietness of the place was getting on her nerves. 'My mother abused me,' she added. 'At the hospital they had dances to keep us amused. The Ball of the Mad.'

She looked at the head waiter, and she and her boyfriend began to laugh uncontrollably. When the elaborately architectural patisseries and ices arrived they fed one another and ignored me. They fed one another lasciviously, licking the long silver spoons and decorated forks, and left almost immediately with their arms around one another.

After they had eaten and drunk at my expense and borrowed some money from me for a room, I went out into the sun and tried to console myself with architecture.

In the Piazza Navona a group of American architectural historians was clustered around their lecturer, an overweight man in an outsized straw hat, who sat on the edge of Bernini's fountain. The lecturer was saying, 'Borromini, who was of a nervous, melancholy and uncompromising disposition, was replaced before he could finish that building.' He pointed across to Sant' Agnese in Agone. 'What he had begun was demolished, his plan for it confused, and the interior wrecked.' The lecturer wore a pale, yellowish suit and he sat with his knees apart, his walking-stick propped against his cantilevered stomach. I had noticed the same group the year before in Naples. Since then, some of them had died. Others, though old, had fallen in love with each other. All were presumably intent on surviving a punishing schedule of visits so that they could have dinner that evening with a contessa, due to put up with them for a short time at her villa for money. In the process some of them had been reduced to using wheelchairs. They were not from the same species as the stone-blindfolded figure of the Nile, and none of them would have seen the point of Velocità.

I wondered, in my own case, about the elaborate manoeuvring of unspoken positions. Perhaps not everything needs to be said. I could not explain my obsession with Velocità any more than the lecturer could explain to his listeners the wonders of an ancient European culture from which temperamentally they were cut off. They were abandoning themselves to a nostalgic ideal from which it was their fate always to be excluded. It is the unstated in art and architecture which encapsulates its meaning, and the unsayable in an irrational passion that comes closest to the truth of it.

I did not tell the trustful Giorgio that Velocità often borrowed money off me and failed to repay it, or that more than once she had slapped my face and head, temporarily deafening me. He would have thought me a lunatic. Nor did I explain to him how the scenes of even my most disastrous meetings with her had become so crucial to me that, instead of working, I had taken to going and waiting around in them.

Castellabate, with its melancholy perspective of arcades and destabilizing shadows, was one place in which I often loitered, hoping to catch a glimpse of her. If she noticed me during the evening passeggiata when she was walking, always in the middle and with her arms linked with those of friends on either side of her, she would say something to them which made them grimace and clutch each other, and they would all look in my direction.

Many people respected me for my work. In some circles I was almost famous. But Daudet said that achieving fame is like ramming the lighted end of your cigar into your mouth when you are smoking it, and I was beginning to feel that without Velocità I was no longer capable of anything. The truth was, I was bored without her.

She was made for breaking rules and for her own enjoyment. Because she wanted only to be happy she rejected everything worthwhile or useful in life in exchange for pleasure. Her ruthless pursuit of her own pleasure knew no bounds. She had a right to frivolity. To her it was inevitable that she should make men suffer in the cause of it. They wanted to be with her because she was easy, passionate, beautiful, careless, animated, irresistibly high-spirited. She felt fated to be happy. Hers was the perfect nature for squandering rigour and nervous irritation.

Everyone talked to her in the street. Men called to her from varnished rosewood speed-boats, Rivas, and she swam out to them and was lifted in. It became a form of honesty, her selfish pursuit of pleasure, and in time I found myself tormented as much by a passion for her faults, and even for her lying, as I was for her body.

She did not love me, and there was no help for it. She would not dream, cry, sleep or even lie still. She was in Neapolitan, unfinished, incomplete, unsolved, undressed in dimensions I could not possibly own. She was a series of events with multiple viewpoints I could never attain.

Despairingly I wrote to her. 'I cannot live without you or remember without you. I long for nothing but you. You conquer forgetfulness.' Drunken, heartfelt, tedious, nonsensical, self-pitying letters I wrote to her, knowing perfectly well that, whatever I wrote or did, she would not love me, would not even half-turn towards me or acknowledge my pain.

Some days I wrote in headlong style. On others I did not use one word where none would do.

'A whole day lost. A cloud of questions.'

'There is no audience. It is only us.'

Some days I was Joachim Murat, King of Naples, returned from meeting Napolean. 'The trouble with Napolean is that he thinks he is Napoleon.' On others I was Puccini writing to his sister Ramelde Franceschini in Lucca. 'I do not think that the body ever betrays the mind.'

'Promise you will love me,' I scrawled, hopelessly, knowing that if I drowned she would not care, and that if I gave up and went away she would not even notice my absence.

I wanted my architecture to be a flux of forms like her, an architecture both very young and unimaginably old, like Rome, of connections, rhythms and perfect proportions like hers. Nude buildings.

'My eyes are so full of you that I am blind to everything else.' She lay baking on the beach. And these letters she dropped in the sea, unopened

I was rapidly becoming fit for nothing. I longed to turn myself inside out to discover what the alien polarity felt like. I tormented myself with her like an animal aggravating its own wounds. Sometimes I felt that I could not bear to live without her, and at others I was perfectly certain that I never wanted to see her again. I was becoming mad for her, and for a whole year my seriousness and idealism were forfeited because I forgot everything but her.

*

At the end of the summer, on a Sunday when pleasure craft left in droves for the islands and for beaches further down the coast, she asked me to take her across the bay.

When we landed, she ran ahead of me up to the grandiloquent terracotta mansion on the cliff-edge where Enrico Caruso had lived, which is now a hotel. Once inside, she kissed me with such eagerness that I felt almost as cruelly treated and apprehensive as I did when she ignored me. Then she looked at me wide-eyed, with that hypnotic, vacant, mad, pale gaze that I knew had nothing to do with affection but everything to do with irresistible manipulation. She was a dangerous and disturbing mixture of determination and frivolity. Her eyes existed solely to make me do what she wanted.

'I want you to include Umberto in the contracts for the hospital.'

'I know.'

'So far, you have refused to compromise.'

'I have told the City I will waive half my fee if they allow me to retain control.'

'But it is necessary always to compromise,' she said.

'To avoid doing so, I have already thrown up commissions and lost many jobs.'

'And now you cannot complete your plans?'

'The jury and experts have awarded me first prize.'

'Yes,' she said, looking unnaturally serious and keeping, for her, most unnaturally still. 'But not the builders and contractors.

You can always be displaced.'

'Displaced by the Bassi brothers and the brother-in-law with the concrete factory?'

'Those and several others.'

Over her naked shoulder I could see, on the far side of the bay, the flash of light where a glass building in the cerulean haze below Vesuvius was catching the sun. It was the only sign of Naples.

'These people would strangle their own mothers to get a commission,' I said.

'Not necessarily.'

'Not necessarily?'

In time, the Bassi brothers usurped the hospital project, emasculated it, added their own pastry-cook decoration to it and claimed it as their own.

I was reminded of what I had overheard the lecturer saying that day in Piazza Navona. I felt as Borromini must have felt when his major commissions were taken away from him. Like him I was uncompromising. I refused to collaborate. Like him I stayed indoors, drawing buildings that would never be built. I knew very well that Borromini, his mind unsettled, eventually became frenzied and botched his suicide.

I noticed that Fausto Bassi, now calling himself Fausto Basilico, quickly developed an inflated view of his own importance. He became heavily dependent on a steady drip-feed of approbation. His schemes – which were my schemes in a newly wrecked form – must be admired or he became morose. If any topic was introduced that was unrelated to him or his work he seemed deaf, and if the conversation was not about him he lost interest. He was impatient of anyone else's views and profoundly uninterested in them. If anything was said that could be construed as remotely critical of him he lost his temper. Even when everything seemed to be going well he appeared angry, dangerously unstable, likely to detonate.

I watched with no interest as trivial architects whom I despised received the best commissions. In few other arts does celebrity fade so quickly. My buildings were not built. Buildings, like ideas, collapse and die as soon as they become compromises. My office was reduced to three draughtsmen in the pay of the Bassi family, and Giorgio Ippolito left, shaking his head. Like Cincinnatus, the Roman general summoned from ploughing fields to lead his city to victory, he returned to his farm.

Velocità taunted me with men her own age and seldom came near me. She had achieved her end without difficulty. I wandered about, not so much grief-stricken as conscious that my shoes were hurting me. Pompeo sat glumly in the bar by himself and said not a word to his dachshund. Despite my father's training, I found the effects of disappointment to be undeniably corrosive.

The air smelled sulphurous. Beauty saddened me because it is transitory. The opposite of love is not hate, but complete indifference. And what I understood everything to mean was precisely nothing.

*

One hot afternoon I looked up from my desk in the drawing office and saw Velocità cross the waste ground and go quickly in at the side door of Y. Y. Laing's studio.

Standing on the pavement opposite was the cousin from Venice. As always, he looked prosperous. His thin hair was combed back and he wore his jacket over his shoulders.

At that moment a membrane of grief burst in my brain, and I have no memory of what I did next.

When the blackness cleared I found myself in the men's washroom of the Modena Hotel, looking in the mirror, and the word 'enantiomorph' was in my mind. As my face came into focus I said the word over to myself several times. Enantiomorph. My left eye, I thought, is an exact enantiomorph of my right. In the mirror I am myself in reverse, unchanged but interchanged, myself but not myself. I washed my hands carefully, my right hand an exact enantiomorph of my left in the mirror, and then I walked back to my office in the site-hut.

I began to draw. My drawing hand did not shake, and my clothes betrayed no signs that I had exerted myself. But I thought, one day I will drop down in the street. The heart, a muscle with two ears and two stomachs, will simply go out of business.

Y. Y. Laing came in and stood, looking at me.

'What?' I asked.

'You don't know?'

'Know what?' I said.

'About Velocità.'

'What about her?'

'That she was attacked.'

I looked down at my clean hands.

'Is she dead?' I asked.

'No,' he said, 'she is not yet dead, though it is a possibility.'

'And where did this attack happen?'

'It happened in my dark-room.'

I waited for him to go on. I was thinking of the blackness.

Without raising his voice, he said, 'A rag with developing fluid, potassium cyanide, was held over her nose and mouth. She has not recovered consciousness.'

'Who found her?'

'I did,' Y. Y. Laing said. 'I and Marcello Carfazzi.'

'Who is Carfazzi?'

'He is the Carmelite cardinal at San Pasquale. I had been photographing him there. We found her on our return to the studio.'

'It must,' I said, 'have been a shock for you.'

I knew it was a foolish thing to say. In my mind's eye I saw, not Velocità, but the long barrel-vaulted chamber in which Y. Y. Laing had no doubt photographed Marcello Carfazzi behind the church of San Pasquale.

'Have you left the site-hut today?' Y. Y. Laing asked me.

'I went to the Hotel Modena this afternoon.'

'Fausto Bassi and the other draughtsmen say you did not leave your work.'

'Then they cannot have seen me.'

He looked at me, sceptically but not without sympathy.

After a time he said, 'It looks bad for you. Everyone knows about your obsession with Velocità. But, as long as you omit to mention the cousin from Venice, it is possible that the brigadiere will have his own ideas about suspects. And there is always *strozzamento di amanti*.'

'It is kind of you to say so.'

'This has nothing to do with kindness. The police and judicial systems regard honour killings as private affairs. Most cases do not get to court, even if they are reported.'

'Is that so?'

'Haven't you anything to say about it?'

'No.'

'Not even about Velocità?'

'Biography is the sieve through which our lives fall.'

Y. Y. Laing smiled bleakly. 'You have always understood next to nothing about Naples,' he said. 'Even you must have heard of *omertà*.'

Then he added, 'But I suppose it is possible she will not die.'

★

With a Neapolitan sense of opera, Y. Y. Laing was commissioned to take votive photographs of Velocità and her family.

The Bassi, mostly minor hoodlums and racketeers, were lined up round her in postures of supplication, their hands raised in prayer. These were men on easy terms with public and private embezzlement, corruption and blackmail – hired killers even – who had never told the truth in their lives. Using a double negative, Y. Y. Laing included an image of Christ on the cross, which hovered miraculously above Velocità and her brothers as if to prefigure a miracle of merciful healing, of the kind shown in old votive paintings. Velocità herself was propped, unconscious, at the centre of the group. She wore an elaborate white lace dress and lay on a bed of lilies.

For the first time in her life she would not be blurred.

But Y. Y. Laing did an odd thing. He set up his big brass and wood Gandolfi camera on its stand as he always did, but instead of taking a long exposure he used a phosphorous flash. As the bulb popped, Velocità's eyes flicked open for a split second, just long enough for the photograph. They then re-closed, as it turned out, forever.

Urged on by Y. Y. Laing, I began in a half-hearted way to entertain hopes of departure. I was assailed by images of trains bursting out of termini and of tall-hulled liners clearing the docks, but Naples had not quite yet completed my humiliation.

I was on the road by the docks, and had just stepped off a tram when another suddenly appeared from behind it and knocked me down.

I lay in the sun, as I had expected to happen, while a ring of faces peered down at me for a time, and then dispersed. The buildings on the other side of the road were bent by my vision, so that they looked like an apartment block by Gaudi. I had no identification on me, and found that I could not speak.

After an argument between the carabinieri and the driver of an ambulance about who would pay my fare, I was taken across the city to the Suore Benedittine di Montevergine Hospital, the hospital for which I had lost the contract. The Bassis' re-building work was not complete, and wards and corridors were full of cement dust. The option that I had negotiated for the building to be on higher ground had been allowed to lapse, and the hospital was stifling. None of the windows opened.

Like all derelicts, on admission I was given a number, being nameless, and put in a ward with additional mattresses crammed between the beds. Double rows of old people, coughing and gasping, stretched as far as the eye could see. In the evening a nun went up and down the rows, sprinkling the bodies with holy water which smelled of formaldehyde.

Y. Y. Laing came to identify me eventually, and I was discharged. But not before I had reflected for a long time on the architecture of the womb, the room and the coffin; and on how ruined human beings are first patched up, then knocked down and cleared away, like buildings, to make room for others.

16

'Why Sicily?' Giorgio Ippolito said. 'I have not been keeping you alive just so that you can go to Sicily.'

While being nursed by Giorgio outside Naples, I had read four books by Mrs Arvold Cole about her garden. It is not an exaggeration to say that these books reminded me that life is worth living.

'There is no great danger,' I assured Giorgio. 'If they still wanted to kill me, they would have tried again.'

Mrs Arvold Cole had been kind to me when she stayed each year at the Menton hotel. In her first volume there was a black and white photograph of me as a child, looking up at her, my arms round a dog, which had been taken in a garden at Vintimiglia. She appeared old even then, fox-faced, holding some flowers, and with a piece of material over her shoulders she wore to keep off the sun.

The books were in English. They had come out, in their matching green covers, about every third year, until drawing to a close with a valedictory essay about the philosophy of gardening five years ago. Mrs Cole much disliked garden photography. 'It misses the point,' she wrote. All her late books were unillustrated. In them she described making an extensive garden somewhere in Italy, and the pleasure and consolation she derived from it now that it had an existence of its own.

In the process she provided clues to her own tormented life in a series of footnotes to her observations on plants and trees. The books and garden were unorthodox. She seemed to understand that what she was doing was without point or usefulness, and that it was tragically transient. To me this made them, and her, irresistible.

Nowhere did she give away the location of the garden, but her London publisher told me that she had lived for more than twenty years in Sicily, at Randazzo. I realized that the references she made to dark rocks and potassium-rich soil might mean that she was gardening on what had once been lava.

I wrote to her twice but received no reply. The publisher assured me that Mrs. Arvold Cole was still alive and in receipt of royalties, so as soon as I was mobile I went to find her.

Her town was extremely quiet, dead almost. The streets were paved with shiny black stone, and the houses had heavy black stone balconies. The run-down churches were striped black and white with courses of lava. Silence, which filled every public space, was the silence of black and white film.

Dominating the town was the smoking volcano, its eye leaking. A sulphurous black cloud hung between the houses and the sun. The cone manufactured cloud which evolved gradually from one shape to another, first into a gigantic umbrella pine and then, tearing slowly and dropping ash, into a series of black veils which drifted off to hang heavily over Catania, or north east across the narrow sea in the direction of Reggio di Calabria on the mainland.

'*Dov'è*, where is the English woman, Mrs. Arvold Cole?' I asked a bartender in an empty bar, but the man only shrugged his shoulders. Among the bottles behind the counter were jars which each contained a dead snake, coiled, and striped black and white like the churches.

When I eventually found the house in the Corsa Bellini, it was blurred and sad like a building in an etching. The blinds were down against the blotted-out sun.

'*Vai via!* Go away,' a voice said from the interior when I knocked.

I went away and bought a bunch of red gladioli, the only flowers I could find, and returned, intending to hand them in. This time the door opened after a long pause.

'I wrote to you,' I said, and gave my name. A hand, very small, like a child's hand but blotched with age, came out and grasped the flowers, but I did not see a face.

'*Cosa vuoi da noi?* What do you want with us? *Perchè ti piagerebbe conoscerci?* Why do you want to know us?' a voice said from within deep shadow.

I was reminded of as-yet-undiscovered people firing arrows up out of the jungle at aeroplanes.

'The garden,' I said. '*Il Paradiso.*'

The door closed again and I waited, but the conversation, such as it was, was terminated.

I walked out of the town. On the black terraces were well-watered strips of many crops, all bearing heavily: lemons, oranges, figs, grapes, olives, nuts, aubergines. No one was tending them. The only movement was that of black butterflies and small finch-like birds which were also black.

A track led off the road.

I heard the sound of a hand-bell and saw that up the track was approaching some kind of religious procession, complete with pall-bearers carrying something like a carpet. They came on steadily and with difficulty over the rough ground. When they were close I could see that, out of piety and respect, many of them were caricatured by old-fashioned clothes of the kind that are sometimes hired out for funerals.

The procession was preceded by a hollow-eyed man in vestments carrying a brass cross on a tall staff. He was followed by a curé in a black cape, a sacristan and a choirboy wearing cassock and surplice. Behind them came a corpulent and breathless man, evidently the mayor, a violinist, and a boy in a top hat. Among the following group of vine-growers, shop-keepers, tradesmen in their best suits, and women wearing black veils, was an elderly man dressed in tailcoat and breaches. The large pall on its poles was decorated with a needlework pattern of tears, stars and a stylized representation of the volcano.

I stood aside. The procession passed, and went on over the shoulder of the slope until it turned a corner and was hidden from view.

When I approached the door of Mrs. Arvold Cole's house on my way back I was surprised to see that it was open.

'Was the procession a funeral?' I asked the extremely small man who stood in the doorway.

'Not exactly,' he said in English. 'They have gone up to place an effigy of San Gennaro in the path of the lava. It is supposed to hold it back.'

'And does it?'

'Never.'

'Was Mrs. Arvold Cole's garden overwhelmed by lava?'

He looked at me, amused. 'They are most formidably accepting in this town,' he said, 'despite the processions. Farmers and market gardeners whose terraces are engulfed say only that the mountain has reclaimed its own. Mrs. Arvold Cole thanks you for the flowers.'

'May I come in?'

'That depends.'

Remembering how precipitately he had grasped the flowers, I took a fair-sized note out of my pocket and he eyed it.

'Are you a journalist?' he said.

'No, simply an inordinate admirer of Mrs. Arvold Cole's

books. And an old acquaintance of hers,' I added.

'Yes, she remembers you,' he said, taking the note and putting it away. 'She remembers the monkey on the beach. You can come in if you like, but she will not see you. Nor will she talk about the garden.'

'Then will you?' I asked eagerly.

'In 1669 Catania and many villages were submerged by lava. Having devastated them, it surged through the harbour and out to sea. My name is Evelyn. I am Mrs. Arvold Cole's brother.'

The gloomy room of grand proportions in which we now stood had almost nothing in it apart from a ruined Neapolitan settle, a dark mirror and a primitive oil painting of a woman attacked by a troop of cats.

But on the wall by the door there was also a small, framed pencil drawing, a double self-portrait. That is to say, it showed two adolescent faces next to one another, almost touching. Each was full face, staring out of the same mirror, and they were identical except that one was male and the other female. They shared the same glance. It was impossible to tell which of the subjects had made the drawing. Perhaps they had each drawn themselves on the same sheet of paper, or each drawn the other. I saw at once that the boy was Evelyn and that the girl must be Mrs. Arvold Cole.

It was a drawing of brother and sister with a single identity. In it the phenomenon of alienation was dispelled. It showed two people as the kernel of one self, one indivisible psyche, simultaneously male and female. The right eye of one face was redrawn, alarmingly, as the left eye of the other.

Evelyn saw me looking at the drawing but chose not to discuss it.

Instead he said, 'Mrs. Arvold Cole is upstairs. Last month the lava crossed the railway line below here. It moves quite slowly, at about 50 metres an hour, so there is plenty of time to get out of the way. People and animals are not killed. The mountain has become very noisy in recent weeks. It growls and, as you will have seen, there is one black plume of smoke and one white one. For the last three years there has been a great deal of activity.'

'I hope Mrs. Cole is not ill?'

'She has been ill some time ago. She is extremely old.'

'Does she go out?'

'She would like to go out. She has not been out for years.'

'Then I will take you out,' I said, 'both of you. If you will come I will take you to the Piazza IX Aprile.'

'In exchange for talk about the garden?'

'No, just for the pleasure of it, though of course it was to ask Mrs Cole about the garden that I came.'

'If she tells you about the garden, will you pay?'

I was so taken aback by the bluntness of this suggestion that for a moment I did not answer. Then I remembered that I had brought it on myself with my earlier contribution. Many people who profess disdain for money lose all control of themselves at the faintest hint of it.

'Within reason,' I said.

'Then I will ask her. Come back tomorrow.'

He walked beside me to the door. He came only up to my waist. It was like being accompanied by a child or a monkey.

'Dwarfs and hunchbacks are good luck in Sicily,' he said, catching my thought, 'though in my case my shortness was caused by a childhood accident. I was concussed so severely that for years I was kept in a darkened room. That was thought to be the best treatment at the time. I recovered in the end from the concussion but, perhaps because of the dark, I ceased to grow.'

From my bedroom window several kilometres away I could watch the volcano at night. The red stream of lava showed up clearly.

I was re-reading one of Mrs. Arvold Cole's attempts to sum up. Each of her books had a similar passage in it, as if she was dealing with something she knew in the end she could not explain. Whenever she did this she went in for short paragraphs of aphorisms.

'The inner world,' she wrote, 'must inform the outer. My garden is what I know but lack the language to say.

'Compared to its simplicity, I am impotent.

'Like most gardens in Italy, mine has two sides to it. They lie next to one another. One is rational, with a straight canal and box geometry standing on logical shadows. The other is voluptuous, barely able to contain itself, in danger of running to seed. I am both these, and so are you.

'You cannot rationalise a garden any more than you can a painting. It is made intuitively. The subconscious is the source of everything.

'My idea in the garden has been to disentangle something from nature and elucidate it. But have I been understood?

'In making it, I have discovered a strangeness I had forgotten.

'Form is at its most expressive when least coherent. It has to be felt rather than understood.

'Colour gives form its inner meaning. Colour expresses something in itself.

'Often I use blue. There is no end to the vibrations it produces in the human spirit. It suggests peace, hope, faith, harmony and a most profound musical meaning. Blue turns in on itself as though forgetting the spectator.

'My garden is an attempt to unify passion and order. I have worked in it freely and with a full brush.

'As Blake says, nature has no outline but imagination has.

'How often in the garden have I felt that I was in my own way, *de trop*, an intrusion, even an encumbrance. Better, if it were possible, to leave your body at the gate like a bicycle to be collected later.

'The garden is a deep idea, unexplained and inexplicable. Its meaning is your own, seen in your own mind's eye.

'Not that I am in control. Now that the garden is mature, it has a life of its own, and the best I can hope to do is to weed out its worst influences. The garden is mutinous, and plants often decamp, re-arranging themselves without my permission.

'Light furnishes the garden as it furnishes a room. Look in the garden for movement, for the progress of shadows throughout the day.

'The beautiful lilac hue of shadow is punctuated by strokes of colour.

'I have made my garden as simple as possible. I think a garden should be unaffected, undistorted by pretension.

'How often I have got up from my work and, straightening my back, looked with envy at the usefulness of the surrounding farmland. There must be something more important and more useful I could be doing than gardening.

'A garden should not be imposed on the landscape. It should grow out of it. The flowers that grow in my borders are the same flowers that grow in the view, in the ditches and in the disallowed corners of fields. I feel that when I work in the garden I am at work in the fields as plantsman and botanist.

'The chastity of classical forms is too mild for me. I have found that I have a gross appetite and relish the earthy. In this way, at least, I have become my garden.

'I cherish the individual and the insignificant. The simplest weeds delight me.

'As well as remembering, I do my best to forget.

'I, too, long to put down deep roots, and flower in managed profusion one day, if I can.

'But there is one other thing, above all, that I look for in the garden, which it may not be possible even to define. It is the incidental.'

And then the passage stopped, as if she experienced a sudden aversion to words.

As I put the book down, I heard the mountain clear its throat and grumble.

Next day I brought Evelyn and Mrs. Arvold Cole down in a taxi to Piazza IX Aprile and installed them at a shady table at the edge of the restaurant from which they had a good view.

Mrs. Cole was a transparent version of herself as I remembered her. The cartilage at the tip of her nose had sharpened as though to push through the skin, and her fingers were skeletal. She did not speak, or if she did her voice was completely inaudible. She watched me with a penetrating gaze. A fire seemed to be burning within her. Her eyes were apparently lidless, and curiously flat and shallow, like fish eyes.

It thrilled me to find her still alive, though she looked as if she might die at any moment. In the cruel sunlight, she was an astounding, skull-like relic of the extinct past, of my past too. In her the past existed and was reachable. To think that she and her garden, both transitory things, still lived. That, by hiding away in Sicily, she had continued secretly against all the odds, had simply gone on, however faded and dreadful, perpetuated somehow in the dark by tiny Evelyn, until I found her. Watching her, I was within touching distance of the lost hotel at Menton and within an ace of finding her fragrant, undisturbed garden.

Evelyn, plainly enjoying himself, did all the talking.

He said, 'Our father was a strong believer in permanence until 9.52 a.m. on July 14, 1902. On that day he was sitting like this, at Florian's in St. Mark's Square, when the campanile fell down without warning after a thousand years.'

We looked out across the bay of godlike light and blue air. In the distance the diabolical volcano slept an indigo sleep under its canopy of peaceable white cumulus. Behind us were the crazy cliffs and bridges from the background of a panel by Antonella da Messina.

A priest came out of the church of San Giuseppe, ignored a beggar and kicked a stray dog. At the table next to us were three men, apparently long dead and escaped fully clothed from the necropolis at Savoca, on whom the waiter fawned. One of them wore the uniform of the local chief of police.

Long after we had finished lunch, Evelyn asked me on behalf of Mrs. Cole whether I would keep a secret. I said I would, and pushed the envelope with the money in it across the table towards her. She seized it at once with a look of rapturous delight.

Then from her bag she produced a pen and wrote in

exceedingly trembly letters on a slip of paper, which she folded in two and passed to me with a thin smile and a long and equally trembly wink.

What she had written was: 'The garden never existed.'

17

We live our lives forwards but can only understand them backwards.

Everyone has his Mr. Marakat, the person who knows more about your life than you do yourself.

Mr. Marakat arranged to meet me on the Biarritz train. He was sitting in the corner of a carriage, and at first I could not see his face. He gave the impression of wearing a carnival mask or, at the very least, a false nose. When I sat down opposite him I could see that he was the father of the man who, throughout my summers at Menton, had swum out each morning to the bathing raft and monopolized it. Then I realized that it was not his father but the same man grown older.

He at once began to speak with the enthusiasm of a Marseillaise eating bouillabaisse.

'What interests me is disquiet,' he said. 'Chance controls more than half of all events. Our lives are filled with chance events which shape them, but fragments connect and relate, and I will tell you how.'

I have drifted into a medium in which I can never belong, I said to myself.

'The amoeba does not reproduce,' he went on. 'It splits into two identical parts.'

'Happy people have no history,' I protested. 'It is a French proverb. And life is lived best when there is no story to tell.'

'I know, but think of two, twin, twain, doubles, duplicity, mirrors.'

'I think of little else,' I said.

'You do not know, as yet, what is missing, though you feel the lack.'

'It is true,' I said, 'that all my life I have felt the heavy presence of an absence.'

We heard the door of the next compartment open and a woman's voice said brightly, 'Pauline is coming and one or two others.' Then the door shut again.

Mr. Marakat said, 'There is a man progressing down the train taking names. What will you tell him?'

'That I am not myself. That I have never been myself. That I inhabit a false self.'

'No, you are not yourself. But,' said Mr. Marakat with supreme satisfaction, 'I know who you are.'

'Is it possible to know anything for certain?'

'I believe so, though there are occasions in biography and history when the facts do not exactly tell the truth.'

Having started in a rush, he paused. The pause was so long you could have smoked a whole cigarette in it.

'If the blues were whisky,' I said, to break the silence, 'I would stay drunk all the time.'

'There are important things to tell you, and I am finding it hard to begin. I will start with the death of your step-father.'

'My step-father?'

'The man you thought was your father, the civil engineer. He died a fortnight ago.'

'I was in Sicily.'

'No one knew where you were.'

I felt nothing. 'So he is dead,' I said. 'Being with him was like being dropped in a vat of acid.'

'I know. I saw how he treated you at Menton.'

'You were watching?'

'Yes. Every day I was on the bathing raft, watching.'

'Why?'

'I will tell you why in a moment. I suppose you realize that it was your step-father who stopped the Menton train. Stopped it in the sense that it was his civil engineering company's blasting which caused the rock-fall on the line.'

'What else?'

'It was he who designed and built the road-widening scheme which led to the demolition of the hotel, and to the loss of the livelihoods of Pascal, Madame Pizzechemi and the others. When his shutters were closed in the afternoons, he was in his room plotting their destruction.'

I looked out of the window. The sky was bruised behind the mountains and it was beginning to rain.

'And now,' I said, 'you are going to tell me who my mother was, and how she died.'

'She did not die.'

'My father – that is my step-father – told me she had drowned.'

'He lied to you. Listen very carefully. Your mother is an Englishwoman. When extremely young, she fell in love with a Greek. By him she had illegitimate twins, you and your identical brother. Your twin was identical to you except that he had a squint. Shortly after that, she married your step-father.

'This was in wartime Biarritz. The Vichy government was persecuting Jews. Those commandeering food were getting rich, and people were being taxed to help the Germans. There was construction work in the south, and your step-father had many lucrative engineering contracts.

'Then, on November 11, 1942, Hitler ordered that all Vichy France was to be occupied, with areas of command enforced by army police. There was increased food rationing. Men were taken away for slave labour, as they had been in the north. The big Biarritz hotels were requisitioned by the Gestapo and the area became an occupied zone.

'I, too, lived in Biarritz at this time and was your mother's lover, but she was unstable. The circumstances were very terrible for her, and perhaps she was always deranged. You and your brother were more than she could bear. Her head was full of all kinds of nonsense, superstitious beliefs and ancient myth. When you were almost two years old, she took both of you to the top of the tallest of the Roches de la Vièrge, the altar-like stacks which stand just off the beach, and threw you into the sea. She was sacrificing you, like the Aztecs. I saw what happened and succeeded in grabbing you. You were under water. It was shallow, but the undertow as the waves and shingle drew back was appalling. The beach was sucked down and seemed to give way. I failed to find your brother.

'Your mother, paid for by your step-father, was put into a hospital for the criminally insane in the mountains, a horrific place full of crazed ex-combatants. Soon afterwards he divorced her. Some years later, by badgering the authorities and guaranteeing that I would assume responsibility for her, I succeeded in procuring her release. But she would not marry me. She married an Englishman called Watson. Your step-father, of course, kept you with him and brought you up. Having saved your life, I felt a certain responsibility towards you and tried to keep an eye on you.'

For a long time I sat in silence.

Finally I said, 'All the people I know have become other people. So my friend Papantonis was my father, and I killed him.'

'It was an accident.'

'And I was tricked into marrying my mother.'

'*She* married *you*. It happened when I was not able to prevent it. There is no such thing as divine justice or divine mercy. We generate these ourselves. Man is nothing but what he makes of himself.'

'I am a traveller on a train going to some unknown destination, and I cannot see the engine. There is nothing to be done. I knew a woman once whose nickname was *C'est la Vie*.'

Mr. Marakat looked at me with deep seriousness.

'I do not at all agree with you that there is nothing to be done,' he said. 'Although man's fate is to perish, he can triumph by inventing projects which will confer meaning on people and objects which are all otherwise meaningless. It is by intuition that any man knows who he is. The terrible rivalry of children works itself out. Make certain that the double does not supplant you.'

'But how can I prevent it?'

'By finding your doppelgänger and killing him before he kills you. It is the only solution. I would judge the sanest man to be he who recognizes his tragic isolation. Now the old shadows have perished under hard axes.'

The train stopped at Etsaut, and Mr. Marakat got out into the rain.

The stinging downpour was no ordinary rain. It hung from cliffs in solid curtains. The river Aspe panicked in the valley bottom. Anything loose was swept away, turning. The river went under, over and across everything. No sooner had things passed than they seemed to pass again. Animals had their wild heads above water. In the village, water poured in torrents down the walls of the pelota court and flushed a wasps' nest from the eye of the war memorial. Green plants were dislodged from the necks of gargoyles.

I saw Mr. Marakat's hunched form disappear rapidly into the station building without looking back.

Now I was to live like a madman and a criminal.

I went on to Biarritz alone, feeling nothing, because hopeless grief is without passion.

18

At the Hotel du Palais, in Biarritz, when I examined the hotel register on arrival my name was already there, in cramped childish writing. Mine was the most recent entry, the ink still wet.

From then on I was treated with obsequiousness and solicitude. My step-father had made me his sole heir and everyone except me had read about it. His company, now mine, was the third largest in France. The hotel manager and head waiter walked backwards in front of me into the dining-room and addressed me as *Il Principe*.

There were a great many very bright spoons placed in lines on the napery, fitting snugly into each other. Enfilades of gigantic chandeliers seemed to have no end, and corner mirrors folded me up from every side like maps. In flourishes on embossed hotel writing paper, Giacomo Meyerbeer had signed his name like a musical score, and written under it '*Robert le Diable*'. This had been framed and put up on the wall of my salon.

From the dining-room windows, and also from my bedroom, there was a clear view of the Roches de la Vièrge standing like wardrobes in an uneventful grey sea. On the tallest of them, there was now a little fenced-in tea-garden.

I inherited my step-father's insomnia as well as everything else. Now that he slept for eternity in Père Lachaise cemetery, I tossed and turned in a bed the size of a house, with gilt coronets at its corners, in the land of the living. I thought, it is important to die as oneself, unchanged by drugs. Nothing is easier than to imagine that the dead whom we have known are still living. It is difficult not to feel that they are intervening in our lives. We see their faces, hear their voices. The living can be, and often are, directed by the dead. Death ends a life but not a relationship.

When I did eventually fall asleep, I was punished for it by a dream, dreams being the supreme workshop of the subconscious.

In it I saw a narrow lane, cobbled, between tall, stone, windowless walls stained with soot. Even in the dream I recognized it. It was New College Lane, in Oxford, the part that runs straight for about 50 yards with a blind corner at each end. In the dream, I turned the corner at my end of the lane and began to walk in the direction of the black gate of New College and the warden's lodgings, with their eroded sculpture. As I did so, a figure came round the corner at the opposite end of the empty lane and walked towards me. I saw that the figure was me. As we were about to pass, he leaped at me and scratched my face, lacerating me with his nails.

When I awoke there was blood under my nails and I found that I had clawed my own cheeks and forehead.

I went to the window and looked out. It was first light and the rocks were standing up to their necks in a high tide.

I thought, *chasser le naturel, il revient au galop.* If human nature is denied, it finds a way round and comes flooding in like the tide.

19

Paris was grey like an etching when I arrived back. There were random scratches in the sky made, not by an etching needle, but by the claws of birds. My mental instability was exacerbated by memories. Crows alighted inside the gallery of Notre Dame, where Victor Hugo had seen them, with little segments of the city visible between the columns. A black horse-drawn hearse slowly crossed the Pont-au-Change. Thunder clouds gathered, ominous and dramatic. Buildings became shadowy. Innocence was violated. I saw buildings from the level of the river combine with the same buildings viewed from the parapet above. A puny fungus grew behind obelisks. I had morally assassinated my twin brother and my parents in the same way that Poe's orangutan had killed the mother and daughter in the rue Morgue. Corruption and the conspiracy of evil were everywhere, evil that could not be burnished out with a burin as lines are burnished out of an etching. To rid the city of this menace, it would have to be demolished. I felt the brush of the wing of madness as Baudelaire had felt it on the Île St. Louis. I watched the coatless, moonfaced figure of Gérard de Nerval, hissing through his teeth with cold, make his way down to rue de la Vieille-Lanterne to hang himself. I lay in the bath in which Marat was murdered. I saw an eel, which had become wedged between rocks in a restaurant fish-tank, scream in the water, unable to free itself. And then the sky grew blacker still with birds. Two flocks of cormorants stretched above the old gate of the Palais de Justice, and writhing in the air over the classical façade of the Ministère de la Marine appeared a pitiless pack of fantastic creatures, which swept down at a shallow angle towards the building: lizards, porpoises, pterodactyls, mounted imps with spears and whips, winged snakes, canoes, horses with coiled tails, fishes armed with sharp anchors and illegible words. A shadow on the stonework looked exactly like a sphinx. The black marble tables at the morgue, Death's hostel, were so overloaded as to make even Satan shudder. Christ walked not on water but on anxiety. Paris was grey like an etching when I arrived back. And then the plate was erased. Cancelled.

*

During the two years that it took to disengage myself from the coils of my step-father's businesses, my task was to pander to my arrested development. It was like having a dialogue with a parasite. I had come to hate that part of myself which I could do nothing but drag about with me.

What Mr. Marakat had told me on the Biarritz train took a long time to provoke a reaction. But Proust speaks of *des relâches du coeur*, the intermissions of the heart, by which he meant the time-lags of grief and love. During that two years in Paris I lived in a lull, a dangerous silence. I was the violin-maker who knows everything there is to know about the violin but feels nothing about music.

My step-father's English ex-business partner, Henry Spofforth, tried to help by bombarding me with anecdotes which he considered had a bearing on my frame of mind. He belonged to my step-father's generation and thought me irrational. A tall man, he would often stand on one leg, hugging his knee in the air. It was a habit he had. He always talked earnestly.

'Did you know,' he said, 'that, after completing his twelve labours, Hercules ended up as a freak show? A slave to the queen of Lydia. He dressed in women's clothes and listened to storytellers singing about his former greatness.'

'Are you going to finish my life for me?' I asked him. Since childhood, I had regarded Spofforth as a figure of fun and always took pleasure in unnerving him. 'The job of Chardin's father was to put green baize on card tables,' I told him. Spofforth liked to know this kind of thing.

'Ah,' he said, delighted. 'And I believe Stubbs's father worked in a knackers' yard.'

'It is the shadow that cannot be detached that frightens me,' I said. 'In *The Third Man* the shadow of Orson Wells was often the shadow of someone else.'

'Was it? Why?'

'Because reality consists not in facts but in the impression they make on the mind.'

'I don't follow you.'

I could not help laughing at Spofforth, not least because he supposed me to be me, and I knew he was mistaken.

From his awkward height he gave me the benefit of his advice. He believed he was speaking for my step-father. It was he who had first introduced him to Herr Doktor Scherau's books, *Des Pensées Noires* and its sequel, *Cent Pensées de la Nuit*. Both these books were much loved by Spofforth and my step-father, and they often quoted from them. Scherau was a Belgian philosopher whom nobody reads now.

'Be yourself,' Spofforth said. 'Live your life fully and to the hilt. Do not waste time lamenting the past or standing on tiptoe to foresee the future.'

'Scherau's *Pensées*?' I asked.

'Ah, you remember them?' He seemed delighted. 'Your step-father would agree with him. Be happy in the present.'

'You mean you think I have an obligation to be cheerful?'

'There is nothing wrong, surely, with indefatigable joy, or at least trying to think well of things. I do. It is necessary always to make your life's narrative join up, to make positive connections when in trouble.'

'A perplexed persistence.'

'Absolutely.'

'But why should there not be nothing, Spofforth?'

'How do you mean?'

'I came face to face with nothingness. Mallarmé.'

'I know what he means. Next-to-nothingness. The dailiness of lacks. That is precisely what I am warning you against. No good can come of it. Raking up the past is like trying to remember a name.'

Spofforth was kinder than my step-father, and knew Latin.

'And there is always *Nihil magis placeat quam quod amissum est*,' he added – 'Nothing is so much loved as that which is lost.'

'Yes, but why should that not apply also to the future? You must surely agree that many things only exist because someone has imagined them.'

'Oh, like pictures you mean?'

'Pictures don't need to exist, but I meant life. What will happen makes it apparent that the past was not what it was perceived to be at the time. In this way the future alters the past.'

'You think so?'

'Don't you, Spofforth? Imagination is memory re-arranged.'

'Is it? It seems to me that people are always asking for answers instead of puzzling things out for themselves.' He looked dejected.

Then he cheered up. 'I meant to tell you,' he said brightly, 'apparently you dance the tango with the girlfriend of your best friend. It is sensual, not sexual. It is a small opera. The first part states the tragedy and the second resolves it.'

'How?'

'God knows. I was hoping you might have some idea.'

20

The second act of my own tragedy took place in Oxford.

I went there without telling Spofforth or anyone else where I was going. I read that a man with the same name as me had been appointed keeper at the Pitt Rivers Museum, and I was acting on Mr. Marakat's suggestion.

It was the end of October. I took rooms on the first floor of the Randolph Hotel, with windows overlooking the Martyrs' Memorial.

'A great pleasure to see you again, sir,' the doorman said as I arrived. But I had never been there before. Later that same afternoon an American woman in the tea-room took an éclair from her red lips and said, 'Back so soon? You only just left.'

I went to the museum towards closing time, as it was beginning to get dark. Almost nobody was about.

I went in at the front entrance and up the steps into the glass-roofed exhibition hall of the Natural History Museum. Stuttering Dodgson's stuffed dodo watched me from its cage. One of the museum's uniformed staff nodded to me. I passed through into the adjoining ethnographical museum and, seeing a staircase to my right, mounted to the first-floor gallery. From here I could see the whole room below without being observed myself.

It was entirely filled with tribal artefacts from every region of every continent, the teeming product of man's cruelty and resourcefulness, the beautiful inventions and coded signals of people who had long ago been poisoned, shot, raped and dispossessed.

My double came out of a side door and began to edge between the showcases. He was identical to me and wore identical clothes. I could tell that, although he did not look up, he knew very well I was there. When he spoke it was with my own voice, in French.

He said, 'All my life I have tried to observe people I cannot see. But *they* watch *me*. In jungles and deserts they follow me, keeping out of sight. I thought, I will run away. I will run away by travelling. I went everywhere in search of them but they were always behind me, watching. My whole life I have been lost and in the dark.'

When I did not reply, he said, 'I know very well that they are deciding whether or not to kill me. In the end they will kill me. Now what I am looking for I dread to find.'

'Insanity has worked for me,' I said. He looked up and I could see that he had the claw marks, the tribal markings, which I had inflicted on my own face. For a moment we stared at one another. I should say that we stared at ourselves. So this was my victim.

'Not all disabilities show,' he said at last. 'You can deal with a man as himself but you cannot deal with him as someone else. This room is too full,' and he turned to go.

I tried to detain him by calling after him, 'William James says that when two people meet in a room there are six people there,' at which I stopped and looked up.

'And who are they?' I asked.

'Their real selves, their perceptions of themselves, and each person's perception of the other,' I replied.

Then, far away down a corridor, a bell was rung which meant that the museum was closing. I hurried back through the side door that led to my office.

And my other self went down the stairs, through the room heavy with the air of extinction, and out into the chill of Museum road, feeling that I was now confronted with an even more terrible reality than the one from which I had come.

All that night I thought about what I must do.

At first I walked the empty streets of yellow stone with their shadows of bicycles, gowns and lit-up smoke. At Christchurch Gate I heard Great Tom's sullen note, one-hundred-and-one strokes as the college was shut up for the night. Then I went back to the hotel and walked up and down in my room.

Once fanaticism has cankered the brain, the disease is incurable. It is a contradiction to say that what must be does not have to be. The madman has the same perceptions as a person who is sane. There is no apparent reason why his soul, having received its tools from the senses, cannot use them. I said to myself, either my soul is mad in itself or I have no soul.

It was as if I was dreaming again, although this time I knew very well that I was not. My imagination, free from the empire of the senses, was at its most irregular, irrational and incoherent. When the imagination is at its most free, as when we are asleep, it is at its most mad. All ideas which come to us in sleep are in spite of ourselves, and the will has no part in them.

At half past three in the morning I remembered Freud's correspondent Groddeck.

'I am of the opinion that man is motivated by the unknown,' he wrote. 'There is an *it* in him, *das Es*, something marvellous that regulates everything he does and all that happens to him.'

'But am I powerless?' I asked myself.

I kept on asking this question, and after a time I came to realize that I was accustomed to translating the will of Groddeck's *it* into action as if it was my own.

I am not in control, I thought, and never have been. I am tugged this way and that and seek to justify behaviour which is not mine. As Groddeck told Freud in a letter, the statement 'I live' is only partially correct. It is far more accurate to say 'Man is lived by the *it*.'

By five o'clock in the morning I had sat down in my chair and made up my mind that, when I was free, I needed solitude. The prudent man, far from making his own fate, often succumbs to it. My vague idea was to internalize all external reality, like the bees of the invisible. Outward happenings, the experience of physical life, made no impression on my memory at all. Not even a snail's trail was left on it to show where I had been, not even a trail of slime with no silver in it. Those whom the gods wish to destroy, they first make mad.

Gradually, the early morning light felt its way towards Wycliffe, Cranmer and Ridley. There was the tolling of many bells. I drew a thunderous hot bath, put on a change of clothes, went down the grandiloquent heraldic staircase and ate kippers and drank coffee in the lofty hotel dining-room, full of oil paintings and college crests.

Then, because it was a cold morning, I collected my coat and scarf and walked to the Pitt Rivers Museum, arriving half an hour after opening time.

I went straight to the office and carried out Mr. Marakat's suggestion.

It was far easier than I had expected and did not take more than a few moments. In the brief struggle, I had the impression that something bulky, like a hump or a monkey, was on my victim's back. But this impression soon passed.

I hid the body in a cupboard, locked the door, and went into the main room which houses the collection. In me is darkness, I thought. There was very little light in the room as if it too had faded, but with age. I was struck by the beauty of decoration on weapons and implements, the shadowy testimony of lost generations from every corner of the world, their feathers, dyes and bones, their idols so potent that each of them looked to me as though they might well be the one true god. Higher civilisation was hardly likely to impress them. I opened a drawer and in it were the amputated paws of moles, labelled like fetishes.

All that day I wandered about. In the Ashmolean there was an ancient Egyptian hand, still with a ring on its finger. There I saw the last blue dreamlike Claude with its wooded landscape of indescribable beauty, and remembered that many experts are not impressed by a painting unless it is totally meaningless.

I found that I was crying. The picture was too much for me. The powdery blue Claude, in which feelings, foliage, water, distance and the strangely attenuated figures in their dream of mist smudged by blurred eye-sight (he was 80 when he painted it), made me sob under my breath, 'Forgive me. Forgive me', as all my sensibilities were overwhelmed. I cry easily in front of works of art. A single musical chord can reduce me to tears. Confronted by profound beauty I am defenceless.

I was in no hurry. Slowly, as though beckoning for my attention, an idea was forming in my mind of what I would do.

That night was All Souls' night. I went into Magdalen College chapel and heard them read an interminable list of the dead. I thought about the roll-call of the dead. A woman in a black veil, looking like a Goya, sang 'Deliver me, O Lord, from eternal death'. Later the choir sang, in Latin, 'Deliver the souls of the dead from punishment in the inferno and from the infernal lake'. There was a thick darkness over the land, a darkness which might be felt. And then there were the mad harmonies and crazy key-changes of the murderer Gesualdo. All music seemed sad, plangent, to me, but now even the major key conveyed inexpressible sorrow. The concealed ingenuity of sacred polyphony invaded, with effortless serenity, my last resources. Tallis's melancholy *Spem in Alium* left me helpless. Against a 40-part motet who can resist?

I thought, in Mexico all the graves will be empty and all the valleys choked with the legions of the dead. I walk in the valley of the shadow of death. I have joined the great majority.

After this I ate and drank in the panelled back room of the Eagle and Child, returned to my hotel and immediately fell into a dreamless sleep which lasted the whole night.

Over the next few weeks I worked unhurriedly in the small room next to the office in which artefacts are conserved, locking the door each evening. I knew that, as my double had been, I was by now a familiar figure going in and out of the museum, and his reputation for shyness and isolation stood me in good stead.

Fortunately, as the end of the Michaelmas Term approached, there were very few people about. The only precautions I took were to discontinue the cleaning woman, and to obtain from the janitor the conservation-room keys. I lived at the Randolph Hotel.

As I settled to my work, I became increasingly confident that I would not be interrupted. I felt no guilt, no remorse, no joy. I seemed to have no feelings at all.

Gradually I dismembered the body and systematically disposed of each limb and organ with the use of heat, acids, quicklime and sand. I felt no disgust at touching them. The dried parts were no more repugnant to me than the votive offerings, charms, mummies, amulets and finger tips in the next room. Dehydrated and brown, they were no longer recognizable as my own. In fact, after a time their human connotations were hardly greater than those of opium pipes, snow shoes, betel-chewing equipment, canoe-prows, nose-flutes and bull-roarers. Just as we do not know what a spirit is, so we are ignorant of what a body is. They were dead things like any others which occupied that now familiar gallery watched over by the floor-to-ceiling Haida crest-pole from British Columbia. Dead and extinct they might be, but they were not without a beauty of their own.

One afternoon I put some of the smaller fragments of undried flesh in a bag and set out to test my freedom. A gritty hail was falling.

I walked down Parks road, along Catte Street and turned under the bridge into New College Lane. When I reached the setting of my dream I stopped and waited in the straight part of the lane. No one appeared.

In celebration I continued down the High to the Botanic Garden and placed my morsels, unobserved, as though bestowing favours, into the hollow leaves and half-filled jars of pitcher plants, *droseraceae* and venus fly traps, the jaws and throats of which closed on them gratefully and began their work.

When the rest of the staff left and I had the museum more or less to myself for a few days before Christmas, I carefully followed the instructions set out in a scholarly paper about *tsantsas*. Tsantsas are heads shrunken by the Shuar, Huambisa and Aguaruna peoples, who live in the South American jungle between Peru and Ecuador.

It was an intricate task and required concentration, but I found it satisfying. Sometimes the heads of monkeys are used, but if the victim's spirit is to be pacified and subsumed it is essential to use the human head itself, and to preserve the facial features.

When at last it was finished and pinned with wooden pegs, I placed the diminutive object on a shelf with the others in the glass case labelled Shrunken Heads of the Upper Amazon.

Then I cleaned up most scrupulously, paid my enormous hotel bill, using my victim's cheque book, and went to Switzerland.

It was not until the beginning of the Hilary term that anyone noticed my double was missing. Apparently it was well known that he had been ill. It seemed appropriate to me that part of him at least should remain in his museum, and – unless this narrative is published – no one is likely to recognize the third head from the right on the bottom shelf as his. Or mine.

21

Spofforth said, 'Stockhausen?'

'No. Switzerland. Staying in Switzerland.' It was an indistinct line and the telephone was in the hotel lobby.

'Really? I thought you once had a bad experience in Switzerland.'

'I have overcome it,' I said. 'I am trying to put architecture behind me.'

'Then why not go to a country where there is no architecture?'

'Where?'

'Iceland. Iceland has no architecture whatsoever.'

'I studied architecture to please my step-father.'

'You wanted him to think well of you?'

'I suppose so.'

There was a pause during which I could hear someone else's conversation on a crossed line. A woman's voice said something about transubstantiation.

Then Spofforth said, 'He was against your painting?'

'He practically forbade it. No practical use.'

'He said that?'

'No good to man or beast.'

'So now you are beginning again?'

'Who cannot draw the map of his life, shade in the country station where he met his loves?'

'What did you say?'

'Auden.'

'Oh. Did you know it was Gérard de Nerval who first translated *Faust* into French?'

★

Paris. Basel. Interlaken. The slow train, and alone this time. No Guillaume Claudel. At Basel there were extensive brown murals in the station, painted in the 1920s, of the Bernese Oberland. Everywhere, complete strangers. Freed at last from the divided self, as far as I could tell I was neither followed nor following. To me, carriages and platforms were empty.

It was snowing heavily.

'To be alone in snow is to be alone indeed,' Spofforth had said.

When I reached a high village, difficult of access except by single-line ratchet railway, with no winter sports and no traffic, I took a room at a semi-derelict hotel where ten or a dozen other people were staying, either for their health or to get away from something. The room I rented was in a tall wooden house built in the 1890s beside the hotel as an annex for summer visitors, which at this time of year was unused, but I arranged to eat in the hotel itself in the evenings. What hotels have given me all my life is anonymity and a changing cast of strangers.

That first night, I sat at a table in the corner of the dining-room from which I could observe the other guests. There was a simple *table d'hôte* and a pichet of Fendant. On the walls were good mountain paintings done at the time of the First World War. Nobody spoke much. The only person who was not old was a coloured woman who sat with an invalid of boiled and throttled appearance and helped him to soup from the tureen.

'Bastà,' he said in a high voice, ferociously.

When dinner was over, people went in ones and twos into the sitting-room, where there were marquetry card-tables, some rows of faded books in German, and steel-engravings illustrating Swiss domestic life of the 1840s, very modest. I learned that the name of the woman accompanying the invalid was Ottoline Hodler.

I also learned that the invalid had two voices: a normal speaking voice and a hysterical counter-tenor. The high voice he reserved to express his fears. It was the menacing cry of another person, the enemy whose role was to terrorise him continuously with new threats of agony and despair. It was Ottoline Hodler's unenviable task to beat off this high voice, which flapped its dark wings continuously above the invalid's wheelchair like a bird of prey.

It was here that I felt, for the first time, I could make something of painting. My appetite for it had accrued over years of starvation. I had thought about it a great deal. After a period of prolonged unhappiness, this was the very time and place in which to begin. I once knew a man who collected Mesozoic bones with terrible urgency. That was the feeling that overwhelmed me now. I must make up for lost time, and for all the time no doubt to be lost in future. Appetite is a form of desire. In that innocent lamp-lit room, with snow deepening against the shutters outside, I felt the first stirrings of a fury of self-discovery.

For weeks after that I worked like a madman, with my easel propped in the snow.

Each day I went up higher on the train and painted the mountains as though I was seeing them for the first time. Their drama, their enormous acoustic, increased with their proximity. Before, on my walks with Guillaume Claudel, I had drawn them fearfully. Now I seized on them and guzzled them like a dog. My subjects became light and the terrific pulse of nature. I had always believed that the most profound painting should be done fast, and now I painted in a frenzy. The imagination shows things not as they are. Every form must be torn down many times and rebuilt in the paint from scratch. My excoriating method was to draw and re-draw in wet oil paint.

I painted larger and larger. Even big pictures began to feel small to me. My glutinous brush-strokes became stretched ligaments, the surface of the paint tugged out of shape like skin. I chanced my arm. I used sensuous darks as if they were tar or pitch. I painted fast, throwing brushes aside after making no more than a few marks with them because I needed the paint to be clean and could not pause to wipe them. I was led to extremes. Often I worked helplessly in a soup of oil and turpentine in which images seemed to come and go. I watched hungrily for accidents, for drips and wipings-out on which it might be possible to capitalize.

The more I stared at them, the more the mountains terrified

me with their bulk. I wanted, for a fully human art, to paint human figures too, in a mountain setting. To have human warmth I needed living people, but I could not invent them. They would not come from my imagination. Occasionally I saw a figure below me, on a distant path like a smear of yellow chicken fat, and painted it rapidly in. I painted it as if it was lying down, or as if it was its own shadow. And, as often as not, I moved it or dashed it out again. If anything was to be humane in the paintings it must be the mountains themselves, done from the motif.

I improvised. A whole graveyard I dug behind each canvas. Like clearing snow with a shovel, I did my best to clear away everything I thought I knew about painting and began again to uncover the truth about it from first principles. I tried to put everything in: love, ugliness, loneliness, tenderness, absurdity. I thought, I must paint the subject not for what it means but for what it is. And I thought, day after day, what is reality if not made up of smears and scribbles?

Painting like this, in a bout of deep seriousness, is like being mad. It does not involve reasoning or rationality so much as a combination of intuition, memory and response, an encounter that takes place in a curious limbo which is more like violent dreaming. In this state I felt as though I was conscious and unconscious at the same time, at least conscious enough to understand that I was in a condition easily dispelled by pausing to puzzle things out.

It would start with lust. I had to have something as urgent as lust to enable me to tackle the idiotic stare of blank canvas, the frightening meaninglessness of an empty canvas so like the meaninglessness of the real world. It need be no more than a lust for blue, say, or for a dark picture or a blinding light one, for an upright painting that was rough and blocked-in or for a horizontal one full of open rhythms. A painting can originate in the mind as a series of rhythms, just as a poem can have a rhythm before it gains expression in words. This much I thought I knew, and I regarded it as the urge to make something without which a painting has no reason even to exist.

But this was little enough to go on. Fortunately, there was the enormous fact of the mountains. Sometimes I started to paint at once, because I thought I had an inkling of what I was doing and needed to prevent an idea from getting away. More often than not I spent many days looking for the opportunity.

Once started, I set pictures up energetically on the basis of sensations aroused in me by the landscape, painting broadly. Although this freshness was provoking, it did little more than present me with the problem of marks on a flat surface which now had to be constantly re-arranged, both in relation to my feelings and to what I could see.

Options and easy solutions came and went. Brush marks worked their various seductions. Of course, anything I altered in a painting had an instantaneous effect on everything else, and every part of even very large pictures needed to be brought into relation at the same time.

In a state of high excitement I tried constantly to use my intuition, imagine, propose, respond, although I invariably had an uneasy feeling that what was happening was somehow independent of me. Systems of forms, combinations of colour, reminded or half-reminded me of sensations I had known before. I believed sometimes that I could remember incidents in the paint before they actually happened.

This middle period in pictures could last for months. Often they presented so many simultaneous alternatives that there was something like a descent into hell. Paintings deteriorated into such confusion and incoherence that I became powerless to extricate them. When this happened I eventually learned to put them aside and let them dry. It meant that I had many canvases on the go at the same time, and each one of them, stacked in my attic room, made me irritable and impatient for resolution.

Six weeks after I began the mountain paintings Ottoline Hodler asked if she could see them. It was her afternoon off and, as it was snowing, I could not work outside. She came up to my room. I turned several pictures round, one at a time, from their places face to the wall and propped them up for her to look at them. She studied each for a long time without saying anything. Looking at them with her I felt acutely dissatisfied. They seemed either incomplete or total failures.

Seeing them through her eyes, I realized that there is nothing admirable about expressing violent emotion for its own sake. Paroxysms of self expression do not alone make pictures, and unbounded self-indulgence carries no meaning. Excess of emotion ends up lacking clarity. I could see this now. Although Ottoline Hodler said nothing, her presence made me think it. The paintings were an embarrassment to both of us. Their violence was not even tragic. The task of painting, like the task of philosophy, must be to disentangle the confusions of the world and make sense of them as clearly and simply as possible. And, in that way, feelings derive from thought, and thought from feelings.

But it was impossible to tell what Ottoline Hodler was thinking and I did not ask her. After about an hour she thanked me simply and sincerely and went away. I heard her greet the waitress, who had been smoking at the foot the stairs at the entrance to the building.

In the evenings I sat at dinner by myself, trying to think of possible solutions, pushing my plate aside to draw on scraps of paper.

The solutions I came up with were partly timid, partly violent, sometimes tentative, sometimes despairing. I drew on napkins, mats, paper tablecloths, in notebooks, sometimes on the table itself.

The heavy waitress, whose name was Pascaline, ignored me. She had a pleasant face, cow-like, with her long hair rolled up on top of her head in horns. She looked at me sideways when I spoke to her. She would stand at the table at the far end of the room, ruminating, and sometimes when the weather was good she stood outside the window, her coat-collar turned up, and smoked. I drew her thick body. I drew the hotel guests at right angles to the square tables in the square room and the square spaces between them. Beneath the tables, where their knees almost touched, I could see where Cubism developed. I drew the invalid in his square wheelchair as he sat, night after night, complaining about his health to Ottoline Hodler.

When pictures had dried, or partially dried, I was able to re-activate them by drawing across them again without getting bogged down, all the time doing my best to make a virtue of what was already there. I have to say that I did not much like this process because what I longed for above all was that pictures should have their whole surface alive at the same time and at the same rate, their complete process laid open to the viewer.

So it was the struggle to improvise this longed-for unity that became the final stage. It led unavoidably to terrible losses, paintings-out, deletions and subtractions. Often a whole picture had to be painted over again a last time, suddenly and as it were at one breath, in the light of a tussle which could well have lasted off and on for several months.

Inevitably this brought into play a quite appalling element of chance. In fact I came to believe that a large part of the whole point could be described as risk. Without it there was nothing. The idea was to get back to the spontaneity of the initial impulse via all the trouble it had caused, and to state it simply, as brightly and clearly as possible.

This final attempt at profound simplicity – what I came to think of as the second simplicity – could well seem like striking the picture out. All too easily it could lead to its complete destruction. But, if it worked, it constituted a triumphant summing up. At long last, after so much hysteria, the entire process lay there, glistening with oil, in all its virility, as a resplendently harmonious, lasting and established fact.

My attempts to achieve this led me into such depths of self-absorption that, going about covered in oil paint, I often omitted even to acknowledge the existence of residents of the hotel. I became so exhausted that I could not sleep. I kept odd hours.

Ottoline Hodler smiled at me across the dining-room from her table beside the invalid, but I almost never spoke to her.

The invalid monopolized her, impaled as he was on his own anxieties.

Each meal-time his pills stood round him on the table, and almost every day there was an argument about them. There came the noise of a spoon in a glass as he irritably stirred up a new mixture.

'No. No. Not that one any longer. It does no good. It makes me drowsy and depressed.'

'The doctor explained to you only yesterday.'

'If he did, the doctor knows less than nothing. They will kill me, these doctors. Take a good look at me, Ottoline Hodler. Very soon you will see me no more.'

Frequently, shrieked at by him, she had to hurry him in his wheelchair from the dining-room.

'For God's sake, hurry. My lower half will kill me. It *is* killing me.'

When this happened, Ottoline Hodler calmly took the brakes off the wheelchair and rolled him placidly from the room. She knew that he was terrified of his own body below the waist, and that nothing she could say would reassure him. His lower half to him was a separate animal and intensely dangerous.

'That,' she would tell him, 'was checked only yesterday. There *is* no infection.'

'Then why does my abdomen gnaw at me like this? Why do I *feel* the infection?'

'The infection doesn't exist.'

'Ah, you say that, but the pain exists. The pain exists. I shall die surrounded by amateurs. You believe nothing I tell you. I am condemned.'

The other hotel guests and I had ring-side seats for this performance, seats in the dining-room and card-room from which we could hear him arguing himself into the grave. In the process, he reminded us that birth is the beginning of death, that illness is the predicament of all other predicaments, and that all human activity is insecure. And yet I think most of us realized that there was nothing essentially the matter with him – nothing, that is, except a disgust for his own body that led him to invent for himself one medical crisis after another, one difficulty after another, because he was addicted to worry. So great was his self-pity that there was no room left for pity to be shown him by anyone else.

He had his own kind of exasperation and I had mine. He would die of fear. Both of us knew that nothing is achieved without fanaticism.

Frequently I was in despair, but in my case there were also miraculous births, though they occurred very rarely. I did my best to convince myself that I was never as bad at painting as I thought I was on my bad days, and never as good as I thought I was on my good days. I painted at every session until it was almost dark because there was always an outside chance that a revelation might yet present itself. I continued to destroy pictures with the same heightened anxiety in which they were made, scraping them off in disgust and self-loathing.

But when on rare occasions a painting was going well or I chanced on a happy solution, it could become a truthful chart of my sensations, a diagram of my own nervous system. For a brief moment I recognized myself in the paint as surely as if I looked in a mirror.

The weather broke. For a further two weeks I went on painting outside because, in my ignorance, I believed I could get the behaviour of clouds to shoulder its enormous way into unstable pigment.

Finally, when it became impossible to continue any longer, I waited in my room in a fever of frustration. I kept the paintings face to the wall because the sight of them aroused in me almost uncontainable nervous excitement, not least because no more than a handful of them were finished. They were simply abandoned.

In the dining-room and card-room I continued to endure,

with the other residents, the invalid's nightly abuse of Ottoline Hodler.

'I was not always like this,' he would shriek. 'Time has disfigured me. I have become unrecognizable, even to myself. I am eroded. Once I may have been almost happy. If so, I did not know it. Once I may even have been normal. I awoke this morning in the belief that I was a child, and was horrified to remember otherwise.'

It was easy to see that he had corrupted his character with years of imaginary illness. His self-absorption was all-consuming. For Ottoline Hodler he had no consideration at all. He did not make any attempt to know her, and hardly considered that she had a life of her own. He seemed to think that as well as buying her help he was paying for her affection.

Then it came to be the end of December and there was that uneasy vacuum, the half-hearted procession of time between Christmas and the New Year, New Year when, in Switzerland, locals in national costume come clonking giant cowbells through deaf hotel dining-rooms, collecting money.

During this period there were suddenly three successive clear days on which I was able to resume painting in the open. The mountains, under their glittering load of deep snow, were at their most inordinately beautiful. And, on the third of these fine days, Ottoline Hodler shot herself.

22

Ottoline Hodler's death was one more addition to what Giorgio Ippolito would have called my *gliummero*, an emotional mess which was becoming increasingly difficult to clear up. Catastrophes are seldom the result of a single motive or a single cause. It was impossible for me to think of her as dead, as absent from the world, no longer in it. Instead I pretended to myself that she had gone away somewhere for a month or two and would be back, perhaps sooner than I thought.

Too upset to go on painting, and for want of any better alternative, I acted on Spofforth's advice and went to Iceland. But I looked on it with a cold eye.

I took a room in a red corrugated-iron guesthouse in a whaling port in the north of the island, on the edge of the Arctic Circle. I used an assumed name.

I soon learned it was characteristic of the guesthouse that almost everyone who lived there was on the point of leaving but never did. Others were expected but never arrived. Everyone was constantly packing and unpacking.

One resident, about to leave but prevented from doing so by some crisis at the last minute, was sitting on the red stairs when I arrived. He was an odd-looking man, his bony face distorted perhaps by an accident. A long face, long teeth, a body with long shanks as though of whalebone, loose limbed.

'*Hvernig hefurõu pað?*' he said, 'and, for those foreigners among you, hello. My own name I seem to have forgotten. Please write yours down. In a previous life, a toast-master. I went absent as soon as I was mentioned. I make nothing happen, rather slowly.'

I wrote down my false name for him, and slightly misspelled it by mistake.

'Oh, yes,' he said. 'There is something not fully declared at the beginning or possibly at the end. But this will do. You have not come out of the blue. If you like, I will announce you as this or that. I can see you have been shaped by all sorts of outside influences and yet are not recognizable as their sum total.'

'Well,' I said, 'announce me as that to be going on with.'

'I will. It may be closer to the truth to be wholly other.'

'Perhaps I am.'

'Isn't everybody? I became a blank myself long ago, a wonder undefined, unidentified, an all-embracing intuition.'

'And you cannot remember your name?'

'Nor anybody else's. I do not consist of affirmations. My name is a stranger to me. A fine state for a toast-master.'

'But you have names written down,' I said.

'Yes.'

'So you are not wholly other.'

'I suppose not,' he replied, 'but I am inexpressibly beyond my own understanding. I seem to consist, like God, of utter incomprehensibility.'

'Dangerously unpredictable.'

'Oh, I don't mind that. Lacking the power to know who I am doesn't trouble me now that I have no apparatus of mind.'

'Having no name doesn't send you reeling?'

'Not if I have it written down, along with yours and all the others. If I get it back, I might use my mind on it afterwards.'

'On what?' I asked.

'My blank.'

'Your name, you mean?'

'Yes, that. But I have turned from the storm now to consider the depths. My blank is before knowledge, you see, and before self-awareness. My blank is also rapture and ecstasy, the nothing which is all.'

When I came down to breakfast next morning, he was standing by the dining-room door in full regalia: cut-away tailcoat, stiff shirt, white tie, and with a heavy insignia on a ribbon round his neck, the spouting-whale motif of which was the crest of the Icelandic Guild of Toast-Masters.

He consulted a slip of paper in his gloved hand and, in a loud voice, announced me by the wrong name. When I sat down he laughed, rubbed his hands together and bowed at me.

'Forgetting has its uses. I have found forgetting the answer to most things,' he said, beginning to eat his cheese. And from then on I was to him the un-nameable traveller.

In the guesthouse the water was sulphurous, the food mostly herring, whalemeat or chad with black bread, and there was little conversation. A sense of wilful incompletion, of something laid down but never properly wrapped up, was pervasive. Throughout my life, the warmest welcomes I have received have always been from hotels and guesthouses, in exchange for money.

For weeks I spent most of the time in my room with my eyes closed. I remembered Zazou saying, 'The hair of the fruitful years stands on end but the water remains empty.'

Then the days became longer, the snow melted and I began to wander about.

Fear of life is a more common condition than the fear of death. It did not take me long to see that what Spofforth had said about there being no architecture in Iceland was not strictly true. In the town there was a green and yellow Lutheran church, some chandlers' shops and a school, with sheds on the quay in which herrings were gutted and whalemeat cut up with spades. The place consisted of no more than 2,000 people, few of whom ever appeared. The single main street was always deserted. Nowhere was there a tree to provide consolation or shelter.

But all the older buildings did have a kind of logic. They were prefabricated wooden cubes, imported from Norway, clad in corrugated iron. Some, like the *gistiheimili* in which I lived, were painted red, and others were grey, yellow or green. Some had a dormer or two or an outside staircase but they were on a small scale, simple and essentially all the same. The builders who had erected them for 150 years would certainly have agreed with Giorgio Ippolito that ornament is a crime. The houses were not so much architecture as going towards architecture. They were as passive as it was possible to be. Facts fell away from them. They lacked exuberance. They made no promise of a utopia where everything would fit. They evidently felt lassitude, and so did I.

In this neutral environment I was anonymous, far from anywhere, all but invisible among anonymous buildings. I went about unnoticed, with no connection to the place or time and knowing nobody, a stranger among strangers. It was a species of freedom. There were days on which I felt mild satisfaction, even subdued pleasure, at so successfully leaving the world behind. But if at first Iceland seemed like a night of the senses, I could not fail for long to notice the beauty of the light. Light moved into and out of physical objects with the freedom of the spirit itself. The sea lit up, and I began to look for the colours that come after ultraviolet and before infra-red on either side of rainbows.

Each day the sun kept to a low arc over the Viknafjoll mountains on the far side of Skálfandi, and was extinguished by a low hill to the north of the town late at night. My spirits lifted.

And each day there was the toast-master, seated at his usual table next to the sideboard on which were laid out the dishes of cheese and little pieces of shiny chopped-up fish. He was the only person glad to talk. My conversations with him were re-run many times in exactly the same form but with tiny changes of emphasis, like repeats in a musical score.

Mostly he argued silently with his forgotten self. I watched him sympathetically. Evidently he had a very active interior life, dandering up, coming over despondent or abruptly sitting bolt upright at astounding revelations. Sometimes he set energetically about seeing off a non-existent fly. At others he would suddenly bite his sleeve. Only occasionally did the internal kerfuffle become audible, as when, one breakfast, he broke out with, 'How many times do I have to tell you? The self may not be reached by intellect.' These were the only clues to how his tussle with the eternal question of identity was going.

'My soul is outside itself,' he would shout. Or, 'You do not see it. The whale is under the ship.'

When this happened, the other occupants of the dining-room smiled at each other. The toast-master was harmless as far as they could tell, preoccupied as he was by underwateriness and living outside life. But as the weeks passed I began to feel that he and I were on the same journey in search of identity, through nothing, to nothing, a journey undertaken without the compass of reason. I could seldom follow a feeling through to full result and might never arrive at passion, whereas the toast-master's psyche was full of incident, constantly dogged by crises and wracked by the most terrible bouts of remorse.

Once, he had to be helped down when he stood on his chair and cried out, *'Ach, was sol lich Sünder machen?'* and Mrs. Elsa Magnadóttir came out of the kitchen in her apron. But nobody wanted him to leave.

It is not what happens but what does not happen that is interesting.

Before going to bed I always ate at the same place, a plain upstairs restaurant in a warehouse by the harbour. Grey-painted matchboard, half-a-dozen clothless tables, a bare floor. There was seldom anybody else there. Sometimes a solitary German eating a puffin.

There came a night when, on the way there, I waited for a moment in the varnished Lutheran church. On the reredos was a painting of Christ rising from the dead in a rocky Icelandic landscape. As I walked to the restaurant the sky was bright green. And, when I mounted the stairs, there was Mr. Marakat.

He was sitting by himself at a table in the middle of the room. On his head was his hat like a clown's hat. He was grinning at me. Pulling out a chair, he gestured at me to join him.

For a long moment he winked at me. He looked inordinately pleased with himself.

I ran down the stairs and back to the guesthouse. Gunnlangur Pétersson, a retired harbour-pilot who lived in the basement, was there. He knew all about Marakat's arrival, it being a small town.

'Who does he say he is?' I asked Gunnlangur Pétersson.

'You think he is not who he says he is?'

'The devil in disguise looks very commonplace.'

'He tells everyone that he is a professor at Reykjavik University, and that he is researching.'

'Researching what?'

'Chemistry. Something to do with the chemical changes that take place in plants growing near geysers.'

'He says that?'

'Yes. He thinks it may lead to a cure for skin diseases. But I must be off.'

'Are you going?'

'I'm afraid so.'

Well, I thought, we are all going to be overcome eventually by the twinge or the gasp. The Gods are psychopaths. I have no clue to the way of the world after all.

That night I saw the lightning wink through my closed eyelids and felt the thunder through blocked ears. With the only real expert on my life nearby I would, like Macbeth and my step-father, never sleep again. Marakat knew only too well what had taken place at Oxford at his own suggestion. And he knew everything else. He was the one person in the world who knew the text and the footnotes of my life as well, the footnotes which pushed the text ever upwards. Now it was not madness but the fear of madness which troubled me.

I took to following him about. In a place which contained very little human activity, it was not difficult. The volcano under the glacier was long overdue for eruption. Everyone on the island lived in the expectation of catastrophe.

Mr. Marakat's movements turned out to be consistent with what he had described as his research. He lived in a neighbouring guesthouse, and used the buses which jolted along grit roads between the town and the surrounding farms. Perhaps he could not drive. I followed at a distance, using a foreign car hired from the garage by the port. The streets were empty. I dissipated nothing in conversation. I was tongue-tied, bewildered, perplexed but not yet quite overcome. I found that one day Marakat went to see a whale stranded on the beach near Mánárbakki, but that otherwise he did what he said he would do and went in search of geophysical activity.

It came to August. Marakat, wearing his small hat, boarded a yellow bus with half-a-dozen locals. A bright day. A double rainbow on the horizon. The bus went along beside the ultramarine sea and turned south, inland, on a narrow track I had not seen before. I followed.

The going was slow. After an hour, we passed mountains that could equally well be small and close or big and far away, with an occasional iron-clad farmhouse, its back to the scree, set far back from the road. In the distance, clouds of spray indicated the position of hidden waterfalls, and once the dazzling sea appeared on its side between far-off hills but turned out not to be the sea at all. It was a glacier. I kept far back from the bus, which was little more than a smudge of travelling lava-dust, pink, in a desert of small stones.

Then the spite of chemicals beneath the surface burst out. The air turned foul. The sulphurous, leaky landscape could hardly conceal its writhing core. In a tormented and unstable place the bus stopped, and Marakat got down.

I parked and, covering my mouth and nose, picked my way towards him across the crust of geophysical eczema. I avoided green-lipped craters, putrid with gas, and cairns hissing with fiercely escaping steam. I was retching. In some places the earth's crust had split and there were trenches of boiling yellow water.

Through all this I approached Marakat who, holding his hands away from his sides, was skipping about in a bearlike schottische, evidently enjoying himself. In his element.

When I came up to him he was squatting at the edge of a crater, scraping at a rock, totally absorbed. He did not see me.

It was a simple matter to nudge him in.

I stepped back, and was about to turn away when the mud and water which were in the crater exploded high into the air, carrying Marakat's body on top of it, spread-eagled as if on a mattress. He kicked like a puppet. Then the jet of water fell back into the crater, and Marakat's body sank. There was a guzzling noise, and a perfectly smooth dome of shining brown mud appeared, inflated, trembled for an instant, burst and retreated into the shaft as if exhausted. There remained only a cloud of steam which slowly expanded over the surrounding land, flattening out into a veil. This took five minutes to dissipate. It was, in a sense, beautiful.

I felt profound relief. The Queen of Denmark once waited for two weeks to see the great geyser at Stokkur erupt and nothing happened. Ten minutes after she left, it went up wonderfully.

I was getting back into the car when I noticed Mr. Marakat's hat resting on the edge of the crater. I thought for a moment, and decided to leave it where it was. If found, it would provide evidence of his accident. It had been most neatly deposited.

It was found. Forensic examination showed that the rim of the hat, despite its ordeal, was still clearly marked on the inside with the name Magnús Ingólfsson, which was that of a missing laboratory assistant from the chemistry department at Reykjavik University.

A week later, Gunnlangur Pétersson came in to breakfast wearing his harbour-pilot's uniform with the shining buttons. Under his arm he carried a peaked cap decorated with rusty-looking silver braid. He placed the cap on the table upside down with his gloves on top of it. Everyone knew that he wore this uniform only two or three times a year for civic occasions.

'Civilisation is a terrible mistake,' the toast-master said.

Watching Gunnlangur Pétersson drink his coffee was like watching someone tip coffee into a letter-box.

'Is this the day of an important event in the harbour?' I asked. 'The arrival of some great ship?'

'I regret to say it is the day of another quite different kind of event,' he replied.

'You are not leaving?'

'No, not that, not today at any rate.'

'Are you sure?'

'Certainly I'm sure, because I have orders to leave tomorrow.'

'Never believe anything until it is officially denied,' I said.

'The truth is,' Gunnlangur Pétersson said, 'I am leaving with you.'

'With me?'

I noticed that his lower eyelids hung down today even more than usual. In the background, the radio in the kitchen was tuned, as it always was, to two stations at once.

'Look more closely and you will see that this is not a harbour-pilot's uniform,' he said.

'Isn't it?'

'No. You did not know that I am also an auxiliary policeman?'

Then, most surprisingly, he used my real name.

'That is my name surely?' cried the toast-master, hastily writing it down on a scrap of paper.

'Things that are not real take on the greatest reality,' I said as Gunnlangur Pétersson stood up.

He looked down at me and announced in a formal voice that he was arresting me for murder.

When it speaks of such things, language is lame and nothing ever seems to mean much. There was a gap, just as there is a gap in the minds of people who do important jobs for which office is the substitute.

'Murder?' I said. 'Of whom?'

Far from withdrawing into aloofness, disgust and disdain, he looked back at me almost with sympathy.

'Of Frau Ottoline Hodler,' he replied.

Next morning we took off from what had once been the seaplane base at Akureyri. A bottlenose whale had taken a wrong turn and found itself trapped in the harbour beside the airstrip. We watched it, a prisoner, surface and blow.

I was handcuffed to Gunnlangur Pétersson. We were on a small propeller-engined plane, and this was the first leg of my journey to Paris. I was being extradited.

The plump airhostess changed her hat to serve tea as the plane droned slowly across the empty volcanic landscape of central Iceland, in which were discernible little bursts of steam.

23

Le code Napoléon. I am taken across the Seine each day, and each day the prison van uses a different bridge. I see the river only through a small panel of reinforced glass.

The court case is unintelligible to me, the whole process magisterially impenetrable. The avocats' speeches seem to have none of the normal trappings of grammar, syntax or punctuation, and no distinctions are made between important and unimportant words. Their barely comprehensible French is like a script full of printer's errors and in a most cruelly boring experimental style.

What is most scrupulously left out is the essential. And, worst of all, the evidence is evidently closely linked to something or someone I seem to have forgotten.

Nothing is more completely unfathomable than the reasoning of Maître Puisat, the prosecuting avocat. His mind and arms move violently. He wears the *Légion d'Honneur* and an ironic expression. His wig is tilted forward on his brow, which causes the bow at the back to stick up, wagging in the air. He and his clerks put their heads together, exchanging whispered confidences. He has a habit of leaping to his feet, spinning round and pointing backwards at me with a flapping gown. So far, the evidence he has produced contains no insights. Watching him, I think: it is not so much a case of what I have done but of what I am going to do.

The three judges sleep high up in a row of scarlet gowns. I imagine them going daily down the great staircase of the Palais de Justice.

My defence avocat, Maître Courbot, recites my submerged biography. He has re-written me entirely. On my behalf he fails to find my true voice. When he speaks he does so without moving, and it is impossible to keep your mind on the actual. Everything is uncertain. There is no point in being realistic about the here and now. Anyone can see that.

'Interesting if true,' he says. It is an event when he raises an eyebrow.

Puisat and Courbot both wear forked collars. The faces of the court officials are a shade of green.

This morning, Puisat says: 'In *Le Malade Imaginaire*, Molière himself acted the part of the hypochondriac, but he was genuinely ill. He took his curtain call seated on the stage and was carried home. He died during the night, of pulmonary thrombosis.' A pause, during which Puisat looks meaningfully at me.

'Interesting if true,' replies Courbot. Like all method actors, he seems to be remembering something else, an event in his childhood, some slight received perhaps, or a hot day in Casablanca, almost anything except what is occurring now, in this particular court-room at this particular time on this particular Parisian Friday afternoon.

It takes so long for the court to convene that the trial seems always to take place in the afternoon. I am tried in the land of afternoon.

'The soul according to Plato is divided into three parts,' Puisat goes on. 'Reason, desire and *thumos*, which is conscience intended to control rampant desire through an innate wish to do good.'

For a moment an incomprehensible gaiety comes over me. Puisat's utterances happen to him as if they are outward events from which he is estranged. I am estranged too. Thoughts will not form into words, and the more irrational the reference the more hilarious the misunderstanding. I fix my glance on Puisat and he looks back at me from another planet. It is the same sensation as when you scrutinize a familiar word, and the more closely you look at it the odder it becomes.

'We choose our values,' Courbot says. 'Morals, truth, rationality are not given to man from outside himself but are created by man to meet his own needs.'

I wonder what Spofforth thinks of him. Even he must recognize this as Nietzsche.

'The fault, if there is a fault, lies within ourselves.'

For days the discourse of the avocats has been like this, half way between metaphor and literal meaning.

Last week I was accused by Puisat of hedonism. 'Hedonism,' he cries, his arms thrown wide, 'as we all know, leads to despair and desperate acts. Thought undermines itself. And what happens, may I ask, if hedonism does not work? Or if it works too well? In ten years' time, what then?'

To which Courbot replies: 'Who said that he would rather be

on easy terms with children, dogs and the seasons than with the rich and famous?'

It has taken Puisat weeks to lay out the case against me, piece by unrecognizable piece. Were I given the opportunity, I would remind him of William of Occam's ancient plea for economy in argument and the use of direct explanations. But the idea that entities should not be multiplied beyond necessity is inconsistent with the processes of a court of law, and we are forced to listen to Puisat's endless diatribe.

To me he attributes a flat atheism which denies the existence of divine justice, divine mercy, or religious transcendence altogether. The way in which he speaks makes it difficult for me to recollect whether I have views on this either way. I am perplexed by my own personality.

He says, with heavy emphasis and drawing himself up as though rearing, 'Existentialism and Christianity are not necessarily incompatible,' and sits down as though some point has been unanswerably won.

Observing the macabre matinée put on daily by the judges I itemize them to myself as follows:

The judge on the left is a terrible old man, constantly gibbering and swearing beneath his breath. Evidence seems to pass him by. He reacts not at all to anything that is said but continues his cursing ceaselessly as though railing against some private grievance. He is sallow, wrinkled. If it were not for the working and muttering of his face I would think that he was sleeping a malevolent sleep with his eyes open.

The judge in the middle is corpulent, heavy-faced, florid. I am familiar with his appearance because I have seen a judge exactly like him in a little painting by Hogarth in the Fitzwilliam Museum, Cambridge. Even in a good light he looks hot and dishonest. His plump hands rest on the desk. He has a gobbling way of speaking and is constantly fumbling for a handkerchief in the folds of his robes so that he can wipe his fat lips with it. Just to look at him makes my flesh creep. You can see that he resents being kept awake. His most conspicuous characteristic is an outward-turning eye like Sartre's, behind thick lenses. Documents have to be read to him. He takes no notes.

There remains the judge on the right. A deadly judge if ever I saw one. Sharp. Neither old nor young. Yellowish and with a sinister, sleek smoothness. Well manicured hands. Yellowish, deep-set eyes. Thin. Beaked. I fear him, not least for the way he has of grinning all over. A grin that comes and goes suddenly, a grin so quick and so all-over that it is come and gone in a flash and is easily missed.

Would anyone in his right mind entrust his freedom to such men?

Since long before the trial I have been kept in the same obnoxious room. I cannot learn to love it. I seem to have lived in this room since before I was born. The same bed, same mattress, same cracks, same basin, same hands, same feet, my same cadaver. Can the body go on without the spirit? Two gendarmes haul me in and out of this room each day to travel to and from the court. The whole vast display of human vitality reduced to this disgusting little existence in the shadow of a trial. So Luther thinks only nothing shall be something? Only the weak strong? Only the prisoner free?

The gendarmes argue every night in the corridor. In prison, you go to a railway station and go on a journey. To elsewhere. To the hereafter. To eternal life. Via memory. Lacking any clues to a knowledge of the afterlife I have become preoccupied with my previous existence.

When they gave me a derelict police typewriter and some paper, I started slamming away at the keys. Proust wrote best at the Ritz. Wittgenstein wrote best in railway buffets. I write best in prison.

The two gendarmes who argue are known to the members of the prison staff as Clothilde and Delphine. They ignore my typing. The loyal Spofforth pays me a visit once a week and I give him what I have typed. What I type is all I can remember, my nonsensical attempt at a dialogue with the dead, the text that you are reading now. I slam in voices and faces, recipes, stops on the Metro, anything I can think of in an attempt to stay sane. I am writing this to you, *cher fou*. An absent-minded letter to myself. Forced to give up the world, I hope to find myself. I like the fact that my pages, almost as soon as they are completed, disappear un-read into the dark. I am putting in all I can remember. It is not much. I am not so much writing as reading my life in a sequence of brief instalments full of suppressed exclamation marks. Born over a grave, it is a letter, or letters, which never got written. My own dark manuscript.

I like the slamming of the keys, the bell, the carriage-return lever. I have fallen on hard times but find myself to be happy – the big old happiness I always used to have. It comes over me in a surge, without warning. Often I have a makeshift memory of some gigantic happiness. Most of the time I am not much more insane than the next man. I like Clothilde and Delphine, ox-like men with moustaches, arguing half the night in the corridor. I like hearing someone playing 'Alice's Restaurant' on a guitar round at the back where the rubbish is dumped. I like the little glimpses of the outside world which I sometimes have through the window of the prison van: a boy in a beret walking on his hands, two teenage girls dancing together in the street. And I like adding to my narrative as the trial goes on, so as to get it clear in my head. Without this it is not easy for me to keep in mind that I am innocent of the murder of Ottoline Hodler. Without this I feel on the edge of proceedings, a listener and an onlooker like everyone else.

★

So now I am forced to re-visit my memories of the mountains and the mountain hotel, and under cross-examination I am pressed to recall dates. By now Ottoline Hodler's death is almost two years ago and what I was doing on precise dates two years ago is a closed book to me, though Puisat does his best to make this seem questionable.

I only know that my time was taken up with painting and with thinking about painting, and that I was so preoccupied with problems presented by my sensations in response to the landscape I thought of very little else. I can remember only too well the frustration of waiting in my room when the weather made it impossible to work outside, but on which days this happened I cannot begin to say, however much I am goaded by the prosecution. Puisat does his best to imply a sinister connection between the clouded landscape and my clouded mind.

Today, for the first time, I am pleased with Courbot.

Puisat begins by saying, 'I suggest that the paintings produced by the accused during this period are irrational.'

Courbot: 'Every man has several layers of reality and so does every landscape.'

Then, to my delight, a large picture, covered by a sheet, is carried into court and placed on an easel below the judges' dais as if it is going to be auctioned. In a theatrical gesture, Puisat whisks the sheet away.

'I submit,' he cries, 'that a mind which can produce this is capable of almost anything.'

Everyone looks at the painting. This is to be my only one-man exhibition. The vernissage. There is a hush while my work has the whole room's full attention. It is consoling to me to see the picture again, even in such inauspicious circumstances, and I can remember making every mark in it.

It is upside down, but I do not trouble the court with this.

'Even murder,' Puisat adds. But by now I am looking critically at the painting and long to get at it again. A useful way to assess any painting or drawing has always been to look at it the wrong way up. I am struck by its rapid drawing and undeniable impact, though I can quite see that, to an audience unfamiliar for example with Soutine, it might appear violent.

It puts me in mind of a place which, because of Ottoline Hodler, I now remember with nostalgia. Nostalgia, from the Greek, meaning pain of memory.

Courbot rises and asks me, quite rightly, whether the painting is finished, to which I answer 'No'.

'To exist,' he says, 'is to be in a permanent state of becoming.'

Someone in the gallery claps, and I look up and see my old friend Guillaume Claudel, the expert on Kierkegaard. He catches my eye and winks.

I am hoping the avocats might now begin a debate on the theory of Expressionism, but here the perpetual hum of aesthetic commentary, as usual, becomes ephemeral. When it tries to speak of painting, language turns out to have practically nothing to say. Puisat makes his attempt. Drawing his gown around him, and looking at the ceiling, he says, 'In Van Gogh's letters to his brother, Theo,' but Courbot immediately interrupts.

Courbot: 'I protest. It is well known that what tormented Van Gogh was paranoid schizophrenia. As the police psychiatrist has shown, that has nothing to do with my client.'

Wishing to dispose of this point once and for all, Courbot has me recalled, and I am given a chance to put my own opinion.

'Everything to me gets itself up to look like pictures,' I hear myself saying. 'Through change, mutability, even contradiction. I am sure that a sense of its process is characteristic of all serious painting.'

Courbot turns very slightly in the direction of Puisat and says, 'Exactly.' He sits down with the ghost of a smile on his lips, and the two judges on the left sleep on.

But it has been implanted in the court's mind that, because I paint with violent gestures, I am – like my mother – of an unstable and violent disposition.

This week there are apparently to be some surprise witnesses. I must guard against a natural disinclination to acceptance. Some of the witnesses will no doubt be called in my defence but when people agree with me I always begin to suspect that I am talking nonsense.

Today Zazou! He looks much older, of course, but is still handsome. He is called as a character witness in my defence. He states that he now lives in Paris. He does his best for me, but is disgracefully and cruelly disposed of by Puisat.

Puisat: 'Why is the witness out of breath?'

Zazou is making his coughing-and-rushing-of-air noise which, until the following exchange, I have failed to understand.

Courbot: 'The witness is a heroic survivor of the French wartime submarine service. His craft was trapped in deep water, depth-charged and forced to wait crippled on the seabed, running out of air. He showed *sang froid* at the time but the terror of it has haunted him ever since.'

Puisat: 'I suggest that his condition is consistent with dishonesty under oath, whatever his record.'

Zazou ignores this and, taking a firm hold of the rails of the witness box as though he is on board ship, says in a most persuasive tone: 'I, too, have my abysses. Out of kindness comes redness and out of rudeness comes rapid same question, out of an eye comes research, out of selection comes painful cattle. Gertrude Stein.' And he is asked to step down.

I believe the trial is not going well for me but there are times when I can hardly bring myself to listen to the evidence. My brain seems to have forfeited control of the many images available to it, so that they crop up unbidden in no particular order and at no particular time.

Each day Puisat and Courbot exchange their irrelevant views on my motives and character. Much of the dialogue has nothing to do with the evidence but much to do with my state of mind. Puisat labels me rootless, secular and anxious, while Courbot speaks of justice, benevolence and decency.

Today I remember that somewhere among my architectural drawings and notes is a manila envelope with a photograph in it. Although my possessions have been searched, it must have been overlooked.

It is a photograph taken in Naples by Y. Y. Laing when he was experimenting with triple negatives. He asked me to pose for him. As in a Duccio, I appear in the photograph in three different positions, wearing the same morose expression and the same hot-looking clothes. As if I am three people in the same room, I am sitting at a table, standing beside myself and also coming in at the door. The room is easily recognizable as Y. Y. Laing's old studio. There is a false pilaster, a potted palm, and a piece of carpet on the floor.

The print has been dripped on by chemicals and is blotched, but the image is clear. On the back he has written in pencil, in Italian: 'The lover, the genius and the murderer, Naples,' and then the date.

It was intended as a joke, but I should certainly have destroyed it.

This afternoon, Courbot says: 'Morality and decency are two sides of the same coin. To know who we are is to know without question the moral sources on which we can rely.'

He must surely be quoting, but always keeps his sources to himself.

24

I am not the author of my own life. Almost every day new evidence emerges that I was not where I knew myself to be. Take, for instance, the incident of the foehn.

Courbot has an effective way of establishing where I was on a particular day shortly before Ottoline Hodler's death.

Courbot: 'What is a foehn?'

Me: 'A powerful alpine wind which often blows in circles. It can be dangerous.'

Courbot: 'Records show that the foehn blew that winter on only one day.'

Me: 'It cost me a painting.'

Courbot: 'Why don't you tell the court, in your own words, where you were that day?'

Me: 'I was painting near Wengernalp when the wind got up.

I went into the hotel there for shelter.'

Courbot: 'And something untoward happened?'

Me: 'No.'

Courbot: 'Wasn't there an autistic boy?'

Me: 'Oh, the autistic boy. I saw him waiting by himself at the station in the snow. The train had gone quickly down the mountain as if afraid of something. I knew there would not be another until the wind dropped. With difficulty, I persuaded him to go with me into the hotel for shelter. The hotel was empty. How is this relevant?'

Courbot: 'You will see. Go on.'

Me: 'For three hours the boy said the same place-names and times over and over again. I realized he was reciting the timetable of the train service, complete with times of arrival and departure, from Interlaken Öst via Lauterbrunnen, Wengen and Kleine Scheidegg to Jungfraujoch and back. An extraordinary feat of memory. Sometimes he said 'Nexte halte Wengern-Alp' in an odd singsong way, an imitation of the conductor he had heard on the train.'

Courbot: 'And you waited with him?'

Me: 'I waited with him until the wind dropped. On the first train that came up was a male nurse who collected him and took him safely away. The boy had escaped, apparently not for the first time.'

Courbot now thanks me and calls a small, hunted-looking man who has been sitting at the side of the court, nervously cleaning his shoes. I do not recognize him. But he recognizes me.

Courbot asks him if I was the person who looked after the child.

'Indeed, yes.'

'And why did the child recite like that?'

'Because he was terrified by the foehn.'

'And you are certain that this is the man who stayed with him during the storm and then handed him over to you?'

'Certain of it? Oh, yes indeed. Indeed, yes.'

I am recalled to the witness-box.
Puisat, jumping to his feet, is full of sneering and aggression. He has a different version of events.
Puisat: 'I don't suppose that even you can be in two places at the same time?'
Me: 'I was at Wengernalp.'
Puisat: 'And I can show that on the afternoon of the foehn you were at your hotel in the village. Were you there too?'
Me: 'No.'
Puisat: 'So you deny it?'
Me: 'Whoever it is that you have in mind, it was not me.'
Puisat: 'I will prove to you to the contrary.'
And he calls a man who says his name is Walter Baumgartner, a man who leads with his stomach, his face the colour of red cabbage. He sports a green Austrian suit, three-piece with no shortage of buttons on it, and walks like a somnambulist. It is a long job getting him into the witness-box.
Puisat, pointing at me and addressing the subject at once: 'Is this the man who spent the afternoon in question with you in the bar?' and he names the hotel.
Walter Baumgartner: 'By Christ, yes.'
Puisat: 'On the day of the foehn?'
Walter Baumgartner: 'Haven't I told you so?'
Puisat: 'And you talked to him?'
Walter Baumgartner: 'Yes, by God. I talked to him alright. And to the woman. No doubt about that. None at all, if you must know.'
And he goes on to establish that I was indubitably in the bar with him and Ottoline Hodler and his St. Bernard dog that day, 'all afternoon, if you must know,' admitting to having had a little schnapps, 'a little schnapps' with us to pass the time until the wind died down and stopped turning the snow round. By Christ, how it shook up the hotel and put the fear of God into his dog and no mistake etc.

So it is then that I know my double had made no bones about

being seen in the village and in the hotel during the afternoons when I was absent on the mountain. If I possessed a soul at all, I had now to face up to the fact that he had tangled with Ottoline Hodler when I was not there. I am beside myself. It is like writing pornography, this evidence, a graphic, explicit and easily accessible pack of lies, complete with a few digressions.

★

Two days later came the piano evidence. I am in the witness-box as usual.

'The Bechstein?' Puisat shouts at me. 'The hotel Bechstein.'

Me: 'What about it?'

Puisat: 'You play the piano, don't you?'

Me: 'No.'

Puisat: 'I believe you do, and I know what you play.'

Me: 'I do not play.'

Puisat: 'Scales in contrary motion?'

Miming the playing of notes, he moves his hands apart and then back together again. 'That doesn't remind you of anything, bring anything to mind?'

I shake my head. 'It means nothing to me.'

Puisat calls an elderly woman. As she enters I see with surprise that she is a dolled-up version of Mrs. Zitelmann, who used to play the piano three evenings a week at cocktail time in the hotel. She came in during the afternoons and in part-payment was allowed by the management to eat her head off in a corner of the dining-room before beginning to play. She took a long time over it and ate as much as she could.

Puisat: 'You have seen this man before?'

She glances across at me with contempt, and nods. 'You have seen him before?'

Mrs. Zitelmann: 'Yes.'

Puisat: 'When?'

Mrs. Zitelmann: 'Often. In the hotel in the afternoons when everybody else had pushed off.'

Puisat: 'Everybody else?'

Mrs. Zitelmann: 'Everybody, that is, except the invalid and Ottoline Hodler, and sometimes the waitress.'
Puisat: 'And he played the piano.'
Mrs. Zitelmann: 'I suppose you could say that.'
Puisat: 'He practised scales?'
Mrs. Zitelmann: 'Scales in contrary motion.'
Puisat: 'And you saw him doing this on the afternoon Ottoline Hodler died.'
Mrs. Zitelmann: 'No.'
Puisat: 'I believe you said you saw him on that day?'
Mrs. Zitelmann: 'No. I heard him.'
Puisat: 'You heard him but didn't see him?'
Mrs. Zitelmann: 'Yes. That is correct.'
Puisat: 'Then how do you know it was him?'
Mrs. Zitelmann: 'Oh, it was him alright. I had seen and heard him practising often enough before. No one else would play endless scales in contrary motion so badly. Always the same hesitations and mistakes. I have perfect pitch. It was painful to listen to him.'
Puisat: 'And where were you?'
Mrs. Zitelmann: 'I was in the dining-room next door. It was enough to put me off my food, I can tell you. Usually he started on B Flat. On my piano, my Bechstein with its beautiful bright tone, he was always playing those wretched scales and playing them wrongly. Hopeless. Always an error, a fluff, a re-commencement. It drove me crazy hearing him do that. I, who breathe only to play.'
Puisat: 'Thank you, Mrs. Zitelmann.'
Mrs. Zitelmann: 'What?'
Puisat: 'Thank you. That will be all.'

So she thought she heard me playing botched scales in the next room an hour and a half before Ottoline Hodler's gunshot. It is hardly proof that I was there.

But Pascaline's smoking does not help. She was smoking at the foot of the stairs the day Ottoline Hodler came up to see my paintings. She seems to have smoked outside practically every window in the hotel, and swears she heard me with Ottoline Hodler, talking and laughing indoors. And this in the afternoons.

★

Yesterday the prison van, held up by traffic, stopped briefly on Boulevard Raspail near the intersection with Boulevard Edgar Quinet by the Cimetière du Montparnasse. Watching as usual from the small window, I could see a second-hand camera shop and, two doors further down, a sign which stuck out saying Pianos. A boy on a grocery delivery tricycle with a box on the front stopped pedalling and looked over his shoulder at the van. A man in uniform walked past and then two fashionable women arm in arm. Coming slowly along behind them was a figure whom I recognized at once. I could swear that it was Monsieur Chaise-Dieu, who used to live in the Menton hotel annex. Monsieur Chaise-Dieu who was always late, always untidy, always elevating trivial incidents into great occasions. Very old now, he had a short, grey beard, wore a curly-brimmed bowler, a rather countrified brown suit, and carried a half-opened umbrella on his arm.

And with him was either his wife or his sister, who had always been indistinguishable from one another. I remembered them as small, yellow with nicotine, viperish, but now she was talking away most cheerfully to him. They were laughing. Perhaps she had changed character in extreme old age, as people sometimes do, from morose to animated and sociable.

I could not hear what they were saying through the glass and they were quickly out of sight. And I found myself thinking as follows: I have failed to have a happy and comfortable life. I did not choose to suffer. I did not choose to be melancholy, isolated, *déclassé*.

★

And now I am cross-examined by Puisat about what else I was doing on the day of Ottoline Hodler's death.

He begins with heavy irony. 'So far, you have remembered next to nothing. Perhaps you will tell the court what you think you were doing that day?'

Unrattled by his hostile manner, I begin to speak at once about the hotel sunroom. Y. Y. Laing's triple negative has reminded me of his darkroom, but I now realize that I am almost unnaturally interested in its opposite. In one form or another the hotel sunroom has been on my mind for the last two years.

I explain to the court. 'It is a glazed loggia built along the whole length of the front of the hotel. You pass through it to reach the front door. It must have been added to the original building before the First World War as a winter sitting-room and retains its painted wicker furniture. Snow shovels are stored there. Its glazing-bars are painted green. There is a big German thermometer attached to the doorjamb at the entrance. The room is always full of light.'

Puisat says impatiently, 'Yes. Yes,' and I continue.

'So that the weight should not endanger the glass roof, snow is swept off it regularly with a broom. From my high window in the neighbouring building, the interior of the sunroom was always visible to me.'

I pause for a moment, visualizing the room, and Puisat says sardonically, 'So you were an architect. Have you a reason for describing this room?'

Me: 'On the morning of December 29 I spoke to Ottoline Hodler in the sunroom. It was the last time I saw her.'

Puisat: 'Saw her alive you mean.'

Me: 'Yes. I was leaving early. It was a perfect morning. She must have noticed me through the dining-room windows. She came out to say goodbye.'

Puisat: 'Did she strike you as being in any way disturbed or agitated?'

Me: 'No.'

Puisat: 'So she said goodbye, and what else?'

Me: 'I remember she said something like, "The mountains look close."'

Puisat: 'And she seemed normal?'
Me: 'She seemed as she always seemed.'
I am saying one thing while, as so often happens, thinking another.
Puisat: '*Harexpatnywasa*?'
Puisat repeats what he has just said, but I still cannot make it out. After what seems a long time I pull myself together, not much, but enough to say, 'Will you repeat the question?'
Puisat: 'I said, how exactly was that? I asked in what way you considered her normal.'
Me: 'She was friendly, shy, sympathetic.'
Puisat: 'What do you mean by sympathetic?'
Me: 'She said "You have nothing to stop you now." '
Puisat: 'I must say it is a mystery to me that you should remember this one banal conversation verbatim when you can remember nothing about any others. What is the reason?'
Me: 'What Ovid calls "Goodbye for the last time." '
Puisat: 'Meaning?'
Me: 'Meaning that people's last words tend to remain in the memory.'
I say this but, while saying it, I am thinking something different.
I think: When I was having that conversation with Ottoline Hodler she was someone else. Some aspect of her had left and been replaced. She was less mild than usual. But it was far more than that. She was resolved, accepting, replete, inviolable in a way not that of her usual self. She was the nameless caller, no longer hesitant, a cipher for a melody understood, a harmony roused. In her was strange knowledge. There were encounters, trophies, old gossip, deciphering, the letter that never came, a valediction stripped of love, a testimony. All this in a long soliloquy.
And something about this mystified me because it was I who had become the stranger.
I remember that when we had finished talking I went outside and looked back at her through the glass. She said, 'Don't

think twice,' and returned my gaze without resentment. In fact, I thought that, if anything, she looked amused. In her glance was nothing rational. There was a scribbling without jargon, full enough but nothing quite – the meadows' tapestry. Her temperament went over me in a tide. Without respite she showed me her soul's axle, her entire mind, returning.

And I, with a knocking heart, was excluded from her altered nature. I could not recognize her.

25

The prison visitor calls each Thursday morning before I leave for court. She says almost nothing, which suits me well. Instead of talking, she looks into my eyes adoringly, brimming with compassion. She is a plain, small, middle-aged woman with round-framed spectacles and a generous amount of facial hair. I look back into her watery lenses with curiosity and failure of understanding. She has found Jesus. She smiles all the time in the pleasantest way imaginable, with her eyebrows arched. The aforementioned Jesus has worked his magic for her, fixed the smile on her face and put her firmly in cloud-cuckoo-land. Nothing that ever happens can possibly trouble her now. Something wrong with the ductless glands, the endocrinal glands, is usually the cause of excessive facial hair in women. Religion seems to have made her, in her own shy way, depressingly cheerful. And the Jesus who looks after her so beautifully, she knows, will take care of me too.

She leaves me tracts. She firmly believes in my innocence. She also leaves me prayers and sometimes a biscuit or two to go with them. I appreciate this. Out of deference to her I read the prayers through. Among other things they say:

> Hold Thou me up, lest I sink.
> Let not the waves overwhelm me.
> When Satan would have me and sift me as wheat, do Thou pray for me that I may fight against him.

Thou has bidden me to resist the devil, but I have no power to do so except it be given me from above.
Look down with compassion upon me, Thy sinful creature.
Be with those who are gone forth to labour in distant lands. As they bear the burden and the heat of the day, may their souls be refreshed.

She is exceedingly shy. She sits stiffly upright, her hands in her lap, smiling, at the same time contemplative, *recueilli*. She could be a nun from the Sisters of Charity at Meudon. She could wear their starched cornette or headdress. Instead she has hair parted like the Red Sea, and a beatific expression. She has no need to be a nun. She is on good terms with Moses, Ezekiel, Shadrach and Abednego. She is no more and no less than herself and she trusts implicitly, unconditionally, in some part of me which she somehow knows to be good.

Meanwhile the policemen loosen their belts, ease their holsters, and go at it with extraordinary vigour. Clothilde and Delphine certainly swear in capital letters. It is a privilege to hear them. Vituperative, scatological, full of loathing, they yell themselves hoarse. They argue so often and at such a pitch that I suppose at some deep level it must make them happy. Their almighty rows are a farcical equivalent of what happens every day in court, a profane version of the lawyers' discourse. *Alors*. I know which I prefer.

26

Courbot mentions the name of a station or halt. It consists of no more than a small ticket-office and a wooden shed. There is a hut for tools needed for work on the line, and a snow-plough in a siding.

Me: 'I took the train up the mountain and got off at the second stop.' (We are now talking about December 29, almost two years ago). 'I collected my easel and painting bag from the ticket office, where I had left them the night before. I then climbed down below the railway-line, beneath the viaduct, and went up the path to the next ridge, to the place at which I had been painting on the previous two days.'

In my mind's eye I see the enormous, glittering snow peaks, glaciers, ice-needles and motionless sky. On such a day, simply seeing is happiness itself. I smell the ringing air. Flaubert hated Switzerland. He told Georges Sand it was only good for botanists, geologists and honeymooners. I think, and mountain painters. It was Flaubert's loss that Swiss scenery crushed him without inspiring thought.

Courbot: 'And you remained there all day?'

Me: 'Yes, I did.'

Courbot: 'You at no stage returned to the village during the course of the afternoon?'

Me: 'No. I did not return to the village until I took the last train down that evening.'

Courbot: 'I will come to that. Did anyone, to your knowledge, see you when you were painting?'

Me: 'Yes. Guido Masini, who manned the ticket office. He went down the bank at shortly before 4.15 to work the points for the down train. I remember he waved at me.'

Guido thought very little of my paintings. He shook his head and joked about them but was friendly towards me. He seemed to forgive me for them. One day he put a notice on my back, without my knowing it, when I was standing at my easel. It read, in Italian: 'I am totally blind.'

Courbot: 'Could you be seen by passengers on the train?'

Me: 'No. Guido could only see me because he looked over the edge of the bank.'

Courbot: 'I have to tell the court that Guido Masini has since died.'

Puisat, with a snort, springing to his feet: 'So there is not a single witness to substantiate that you were on the mountain at the time of the murder.'

The judge on the right gestures at Puisat to sit down, and Courbot resumes: 'Before catching the train back to the village, you left your painting equipment and the painting in the ticket-office as usual?'

Me: 'I clambered with my painting up the bank. Guido was in the office, smoking, with his feet on a chair. There was a fire in the waiting-room next door and I waited there for ten minutes until the train came.'

Pinned to the wooden walls of the waiting-room are old railway posters, large, sunny, steel-engraved views of the mountains, seen as if through telescopes on hotel terraces. They epitomise fine mornings, health and the jauntiness of pre-war walkers who use sticks which are banded with the names of places they have visited by rail.

Courbot: 'Yes?'

Me: 'Then Guido Masini locked up, and he and I took the last train down. By then it must have been almost dark.'

By then I am irritable with nervous exhaustion. My effort to sum up the painting has damaged it beyond repair. The effect of this last effort is always to leave me limp and hardly conscious of the journey back.

Courbot: 'Was it a crowded train?'

Me: 'I believe it was empty.'

Courbot: 'Empty?'

Me: 'As far as I remember, there were the usual three carriages and they were all empty.'

Courbot: 'Did you speak to the driver?'

Me: 'I think Guido did, briefly. They did not like one another. I do not remember saying anything.'

Puisat, interrupting: 'The driver did not see you. Nobody remembers seeing you.'

Courbot: 'How could they? It is two years ago.'

The village station to which we get back is a simple one. Two lines. A wooden station building with a small clock-turret on the roof, in deep snow. No platforms. You walk across the lines when getting on or off a train. A canopy on the front of the building to protect passengers beside the up line. Attached to the waiting-room is a small shop which sells newspapers, cigarettes and chocolate, closed by this time in the evening.

Courbot: 'So you parted from Guido Masini at the station?'
Me: 'Yes'.
Courbot: 'Now, answer carefully. You must surely have seen someone at the station?'
Me: 'Not on the station, only on the waiting train.'
Courbot: 'The carriages in which you and Guido Masini had come down were then attached to a waiting train for the rest of the descent. Is that right?'
Me: 'Yes. The lights were on in the carriages and I saw a man in one of them as I passed.'
Courbot: 'Did he see you?'
Me: 'Yes. He looked at me.'
Courbot: 'And had you seen him before?'
Me: 'I believe so.'

The lights are on in the carriage and the man is standing up, putting something on the luggage rack. He is wearing my long coat and my hat. He turns his head, with his arms still extended upwards, and looks at me. When he sees me he smiles and says something which I cannot make out. His face is brown. The train begins to move. It starts to move at almost exactly the moment that we see one another, and in no time he is out of sight.

For an instant I was face to face with him. In high fettle he bestowed a glance on me, smiled, mouthed something and waved his hand, with only the glass between us. And was gone.

Courbot: 'You seem doubtful. Did you recognize him?'
Me: 'He looked familiar. It is possible I may have seen him before somewhere.'
Courbot: 'Where?'
Me: 'I have no idea. Perhaps in another country.'
Courbot: 'Can you describe him?'
Me: 'About my age, wearing a coat and hat. I saw him only for an instant. He had obviously just boarded the train.'

Courbot turns to the court and says: 'Unfortunately, the defence has been unable to trace this anonymous witness.'

I think to myself: Yes, anonymous witness.

Courbot: 'The best I can do is to leave the existence of this individual in the mind of the court.'

I look across at Puisat. He and his clerks are laughing.

I step through the snow between the rails and walk back up the path to the hotel.

Courbot: 'And what did you find when you arrived back?'

Me: 'There were some motorized sledges and an ambulance in front of the hotel, and I could see that there was a group of people in the sunroom.'

Courbot: 'The sunroom again. You did not go to investigate?'

Me: 'No. I went to my room.'

Courbot: 'Weren't you curious?'

Me: 'No. I thought one of the old people in the hotel was ill. It had happened before.'

Courbot: 'You watched from your window?'

Me: 'I remember that for a long time I lay on my bed. When I did eventually look out of my window I saw that the police were there. All the lights were on in the sunroom, and I realized that there was a body on a stretcher on the floor. It was wrapped in a blanket, with the blanket over its head, so I could tell that it was dead. I had no way of knowing who it was.'

I fail to recognize Ottoline Hodler's dead body in just the same way that, a few hours earlier, I failed to recognize her alive. I stand watching as the body is lifted into the ambulance and is driven slowly away, round the corner and down the slope in the direction of the village.

Courbot: 'When did you discover that the body was in fact that of Ottoline Hodler?'

Me: 'After about an hour I went down and across to the hotel for dinner. Nobody was in the dining-room. Then the enthusiast for Esperanto, whom everyone called Fritzi, came in and sat at his usual table. Until then I had speculated that he was the one who had died. After that, I remember thinking it might be Ottoline Hodler's invalid because he seemed the most likely of all of them.'

Courbot: 'Yes, but who told you it was Ottoline Hodler?'

Me: 'Pascaline, the waitress, when she brought my soup. As

she put the tureen on the table I asked her who had died. To tell the truth, up to that point I was not particularly interested. Apart from Ottoline Hodler I knew none of them except by sight.'

Courbot: 'Do you remember what she said?'

Me: 'I do.' Pascaline seems afraid of me. 'What she said was "Frau Hodler. This afternoon. In the office. Shot. The mess!"'

Courbot: 'And when you finally learned that it was Ottoline Hodler who had died, what did you do?'

Me: 'I was horrified. I spent a sleepless night and left the next day.'

Courbot: 'But not before being interviewed by the police?'

Me: 'No. Next morning a detective sergeant set up a temporary office in the sunroom. I told him what I have told you. It was not a murder investigation. I gave him my address, and he informed me that I was free to go.'

Puisat, jumping up and swirling his gown: 'And may I ask what address you gave him?'

Me: 'I gave him my permanent address, which is my Paris address.'

Puisat: 'Your Paris address, yes. And then,' (he is shouting) 'what did you do? You went to Iceland under a false name. *Why?*'

Woken by the commotion, the middle one of the three scarlet judges says, in a drawling voice: 'Not now, Maître Puisat. All in good time.' And the dogs of war, for the time being, are drawn off.

27

'I do so agree,' says Spofforth, standing on one leg and nervously hugging his knee. A conversation is already taking place in his mind, one we have not had.

'What?' I ask.

'Precisely what I wanted to say myself,' he replies, and sits down.

He is on his weekly visit, but he is no longer visiting me. The person he visits is his old idea of me. To him I have become somebody else.

'And that is what de Nerval said when asked why he walked his lobster in the park.'

'The lobster does not bark and knows the secrets of the sea.'

'Exactly.'

There is a pause, and Spofforth stands up again.

'Oeufs en cocotte a la crème,' he explains gently. 'Most delicious way imaginable.'

I let him run on. The natural excitement of the brain is finely balanced, delicate, easily disturbed. Spofforth, during recent visits, has become a past-master of non-communication. There is an infinite number of ways in which things may almost be said, and by now he is expert at avoiding the point of many of them. He can evade the issue for a second or two or for hours on end as the evidence accumulates against me. His range extends from little patches of palest déjà-vu to prolonged and violent bouts of non-sequiturs.

'On top of the stove. Little china ramekins with butter in them, stood in a pan of boiling water. An egg in each. As the whites start to set, pour in a tablespoonful of thick cream. Serve when the whites are well set but the yolks are still soft. Most delicious way of cooking eggs ever invented.'

He looks relieved to have said this and not something else. His idea is to sound, in spite of everything, relaxed and authentic.

The reinforced wire mesh between us throws a network of lines over Spofforth as though he is caught in a net. Trapped. But the mesh of shadow also puts me in mind of the confessional, the shadow thrown on the face and the psyche by its grille. While Spofforth speaks beside the point, I speak not at all. What I, for my part, do not communicate is as follows:

The world is mad. It is the task of painting and metaphysics to re-organise it. I have come to realize that many of the questions it occurred to me to ask are meaningless or unanswerable. I wonder now what it was I so much wanted, when it is likely that philosophy would effortlessly show the questions to have been beside the point.

With the gift of loneliness comes the gift of privacy. There are degrees of insanity. Everyone is more or less insane. Even you, Spofforth.

As two people, or many more than two, I wanted my lives to be simultaneous. Those who believe themselves doubled can have fuller, more intense lives than one person in isolation. It is rare for an individual to act on his own account. Even passions can be quotations.

What is aphasia? Spofforth looks sadly down at his hands. He embarks on sentences and forgets the word for what he had intended to say at the end of them.

Briefly he cheers up when he says, 'Of course, you know that the waterfall you lie listening to at night is not the same waterfall that you visit in the daytime.'

'Ah, Herr. Doktor Scherau's *Pensées?*'

'You are right. Scherau, *Cent Pensées de la Nuit.*'

'I thought, *'Des Pensées Noires?*'

What you can never know, Spofforth, is that success is failure and failure success. Applause should tell the serious artist that he is on the wrong track. Cézanne was never exposed to the indignity of official recognition.

But now Spofforth is in his chair again. He tries his utmost to mimic his themes, to speak in a way best suited to his topic. It involves some acting. He looks tired out by the effort. It exhausts him to keep clear of the subject, to strip out the plot and still be left with something to say. He speaks up and speaks down. He leaves spaces. He quotes himself without using quotation marks. As narrator he has the option of letting the dialogue run on aloud and undisturbed as long as it is entirely beside the point. He feels no need to interpret himself.

'And that is how he writes. Buys a tin of biscuits. Locks himself in a room. Three days. Perhaps four. Biscuits finished. Novel finished. Simenon.'

'Quickly as that?'

'As quickly as that. But only after two or three months' research first, of course.'

'Of course.'

You do not exist. You and I, Spofforth, are no more than a few random episodes.

'How many words?'

'Not many. Fifty thousand? Sixty thousand. It depends.'

For years I suffered from the conviction that someone unidentified was on the periphery of my attention. I could not focus on him. Worse than alarming, the sense that I was one too many. That few months of painting in the mountains. The figure on the path far below. Me? On the path like a yellow smear of fat. Me or not me? Or was it you, *cher psychopath*, rapidly catching me up? Surely I was delayed, held up somewhere, late, shrugged off. The bane of your life has either to be lived with or somehow shrugged off. Do you remember how, before Anna Karenina's suicide, everything was doubled in her soul? There have been occasions in the past when, for a few months, painting or working as an architect, I briefly deluded myself that I was me.

Even in the winter, the interrupted, falling song of the chaffinches is everywhere in the alpine conifers.

Spofforth, looking older and with a permanently tired expression, stands up as if to leave, then sits down again and regards me earnestly from within his net.

'The alpine past,' he quotes Scherau, 'excludes the inessential. Take time. Remain quiet. Accept what cannot be changed and change what you can. In the mountains everything is connected, and metaphysical speculation is useless.'

And I understand perfectly that within the silence he describes is the gunshot in the hotel office, the horrendous blast in a small room. Ottoline Hodler died here. The police photographs were shown in court and have been reproduced this week over two double-spreads in *Paris Match*. Her body on the floor but her legs somehow propped on the desk. The overturned chair with the burst corduroy bladder of a cushion. The unlocked gun cabinet, out-of-date calendar, black and white pre-war photographs of a ski jumper and the Silberhorn. Bills, receipts, letters beneath which are buried a telephone, a typewriter. A stuffed capercaillie. A stuffed mountain fox with a scandalized expression. A carved cuckoo clock, door hanging open. All of them are constituent parts of Scherau's silent alpine past desecrated, blown cruelly apart.

Neither of us speaks of them.

Across the yard someone is playing, for the umpteenth time, 'Alice's Restaurant', all eighteen minutes and twenty seconds of it. 'You can get anything you want ('cept Alice) at Alice's Restaurant.'

Spofforth says, 'Leibniz.'

'What?'

'Leibniz. You were trying to remember the name of Leibniz's dog.'

'Not Leibniz, Schopenhauer.'

'Schopenhauer then.'

'Schopenhauer's poodle.'

I say the name. In this way and others we succeed in saying nothing at all about the topic under discussion.

*

Today, Puisat to me in the witness box: 'Esperanto?"

Me: 'What about it?'

Puisat: 'I believe you write, read, understand the language Esperanto.'

Me: 'No.'

Puisat: 'You denied playing the piano. Now you have no knowledge of Esperanto, so you say.'

Me: 'I do say that. I have a few words of the Swiss Romansch dialect but not of Esperanto.'

Puisat: 'Say something in Romansch dialect'

Me: '*La ciavra lis à mangiadis, O missâr pari.*'

Puisat: 'Which means?'

Me: 'The goat ate them, Father.'

Puisat: 'That also is in a letter. But you don't know Esperanto?'

Me: 'I'm afraid not.'
Puisat: 'So you needed some help with it.'
He is holding up a letter which is then passed to me. 'Is this your handwriting?'
I look at it with interest.
Me: 'A forgery. I have never seen it before.'
Puisat: 'A love letter to Ottoline Hodler in your handwriting, and you say you have never seen it before.'
Me: 'I never wrote to Ottoline Hodler.'
Puisat tells me to stand down and calls 'Fritzi' Taube to give evidence. This is Fritzi the Esperanto expert, familiar to me only by sight across the hotel dining-room. A very noisy sucker-up of soup. Like Walter Baumgartner, he appears well nourished.
Puisat: 'You recognize the accused?'
Fritzi Taube: 'If I didn't I don't suppose I would be on my hind legs in a court of law when I could be somewhere else.'
Puisat: 'Just yes or no.'
Fritzi Taube: 'Yes.'
Puisat: 'He asked you to translate a phrase for him into Esperanto?'
Fritzi Taube: 'Yes'.
Puisat: 'Then say it.'
Fritzi Taube: '*Pripens ĝi. Mi êe ne ekzist.*'
Puisat: 'And what does that mean exactly?'
Fritzi Taube: 'It means: Think of it. I did not even exist.'
Puisat, turning dramatically to the judges: 'This phrase, in Esperanto, is in the letter.'
I recognize it. It is a quotation from *Doctor Jekyll and Mr. Hyde*.

★

Last night I awoke in the dark with a jolt. My brain, unasked, was providing edited highlights of conversations I had overheard between Ottoline Hodler and the invalid.
In the card-room one evening he confided to her in his normal voice, 'All my life I have worried dreadfully about money, about illness, about food, about travel, about my childhood, about ad-

olescence, about growing old, about anything and everything. I am terrified of opening letters. Terrified of being late.' His voice changed to the counter-tenor shriek. 'So why should I not be terrified of dying?'

There were several versions of this. At other times he would say, 'When I was a child I tried to imagine the terrors of growing up. Growing up turned out to be even worse than I feared. And when I was an adult I did my best not to think about the horrors of growing old, of becoming senile, of being ill. The reality turns out to be even more appalling than I had ever thought possible. And there is no respite, no remedy.'

I can hear Ottoline Hodler, her days full of the degrading demands of the invalid's dire body and bitter heart, being told by him that she irritated him. He was heavy to lift, a dead weight, and he did nothing to help her. Instead he cried out with fear of falling backwards.

'You should know by now. I always leave the seventh pill.'

And, 'Turn me round. Turn the chair round. You must always turn the chair twice here.'

And, 'Of course I'm angry, angry at you, angry at being ill, angry at dying.'

He would strike out at her, push her away. Yet he was helpless without her.

And what was her response to such treatment? It was far better than plain acceptance. Throughout, her spirits were unstifled, positively resplendent. The trays of hotel coffee, the chicken wings, the fetching and carrying, the struggles morning and evening with the invalid's surgical stockings, none of this spoiled her conviction that virtue is to be found in the everyday. No candidate for suicide says, as she once did, pulling a long face at me, 'I think momentousness attends the perfectly ordinary. Aren't our innermost feelings in the commonplace?'

When I heard her say this, I could imagine the conversations she had with the squinting brother in Christ who was seducing her. He had written to her in my handwriting. The evidence was accumulating. She was counting on him to spring her from her trap. Why else would she turn to me one day, while manoeuvring the invalid's wheelchair, and remark half-humorously, 'So what is life but an accumulation of trivial details?'

I should have killed the brother in Christ on the train. I should have jumped on board the moment I saw him. There is a dark tunnel above Lauterbrunnen which it takes 17 seconds for the carriages to pass through. That would have been enough.

He had smiled at me and said something, signing, tall as my own conscience. I know now what he signed. It was 'Doubles'. He could have been my reflection in the carriage window. How could I be certain that he had an existence independent of me, one that continued when he was not in my mind? How can I be sure that any of my selves, *cher fou*, are other than remembered or imagined? Do I know this in the sense of *savoir* or *connaître* in French, *wissen* or *kennen* in German? Who went down in the train after killing Ottoline Hodler, him or me?

Six months after her death a man was arrested on a Swiss train whom they thought was me, a man with a squint. He turned out to be a priest. He had an irreproachable alibi. The police apologized and let him go.

So, if I had killed him in the tunnel, which of us would have disembarked from the train at Lauterbrunnen and, breathing a sigh of relief, looked up at the dangling Staubbach Falls – the Falls stopped dead in mid air, frozen, as if in a photograph – and thought himself a free man?

28

The trial, it goes on for months, years even. On hot days when the tops of the windows in the courtroom stand open there is the noise of traffic on the boulevard. And at other times the thermometer is down to zero or below zero. Some days everything fits together like a jigsaw puzzle. On others, one moment coming to another fails to meet.

Each day always starts like this: the three judges come in and take their places, high up on a dais. They have already had an appetizer, a little nip, and will very soon adjourn for something a good deal more substantial. Capricious, malevolent, morose, mendacious, all linings and trimmings, swollen with half-suppressed yawns, they file in like a troupe of crazy, bent, ham actors, a row of freaks with cirrhosis of the liver, tape worms, poisonous intestines, blood in the urine. In fact, not unlike the rest of us.

For there is surely a close similarity between the judges and the judged. All men are prisoners. We are not so different, they and I. Each of us is caught up in this same buffoonery, the buffoonery of justice. It is just that, unfortunately, some men have the gall to pass sentence on others. *Homo homini lupus*. Man is a wolf to man.

What is more, I realize now where we have all seen them, this row of three judges, long before the trial began. The one on the left cannot hear, the one in the centre cannot see, and the one on the right – the smiling death's head with the arrogant nose – is the one who speaks evil.

★

Finally, just when I am losing interest, something happens which I have been dreading for months.

Mr. Marakat, alive and well, is called as a witness for the prosecution.

When I last saw him, on the Marseilles train, his nose, chin and conical hat had made him look like a Daumier or Rouault clown. Now the hat is only a memory. It has left its mark in the form of an equator round his head, but he is greatly changed. He looks prosperous. He seems to be decked out for some kind of folklore celebration, and there is evidently something amusing him. He never smiled before, but now he is unable to speak without showing his teeth. The joke is not yet revealed, but looking at him across the courtroom I see that it will be, very soon. Whatever emerges under questioning, I feel sure it will be greatly to my detriment. I hate revelations.

Puisat, after the usual preliminaries: 'Mr Marakat. Will you begin by explaining to the court how you know the accused?'

Sometimes French needs far fewer words than most other languages, and Marakat begins to speak succinctly.

'I knew his family. I knew him when he was a baby at Biarritz. Later, when his mother became ill, I kept an eye on him.'

Puisat: 'In what way was his mother ill?'

Marakat: ' She was mentally ill.'

Puisat: 'She was certified insane?'

Marakat: 'Yes.'

Puisat looks round significantly and says, 'I ask the court to note this.'

Marakat grins. The red face, very pale blue eyes, exaggerated nose, extremely white teeth. The question which he is so longing to be asked will come all too soon. His demeanour is that of egging Puisat on, and he knows that his powers of expression are more than equal to whatever comes up. It occurs to me that perhaps he is in disguise.

But Puisat seems reluctant to abandon the idea of my mother's insanity and, looking thoughtfully at me, says, 'His mother was mad.'

I think of the prison-like asylum with its rows of barred shutters, high up on a shaly plain near the Spanish border. Grey stone. Patches of snow. A place purpose-built for pre-frontal leucotomies and electroconvulsive treatment, with sheds for re-straining hysterics and re-organising the personality.

'Now,' says Puisat, as though pulling himself together, 'I want you to tell us exactly how and when the accused first met Ottoline Hodler.'

He says this so loudly and so theatrically, taking up a document and leaning with it far out of his desk in the direction of the witness, that one of the judges, the one on the right, becomes suddenly alert and says: 'Are you implying, Maître Puisat, that the accused knew Ottoline Hodler *before he met her in the Swiss hotel?*'

People look at me. I shake my head in vehement denial and say, 'She was a stranger to me.'

'Not true! Not true!' shouts Puisat. 'In fact, he had known her a long time.' He whirls round again to the smiling Marakat, whose moment has at last come. Marakat now seems about to accompany his dressed-up self on an entertaining expedition.

Relishing every word of his narrative, Marakat changes gear into the historic present and says slowly, 'It is the summer of 1953. The accused is staying at Menton. I live nearby.'

His delivery is so slow that I have time to see him as he was then, the man on the bathing raft. I see the hotel, and Pascal. I smell the irresistible smells of herbs in cooking, of Ambre Solaire, Disque Bleu and cigar smoke. I think how much, as a child, I longed to have conversations with people older than myself. In an abrupt convulsion of memory, I am young and remember the violence of my serenity, the happiness of living in the imagination, of re-inventing life every day. I can draw on a fish. The surface of the world is no more terrifying than the surface of a melon. Everything is outsize sculpture to an ant. Pencil-lines live on the seabed and form sentences when caught in nets. Hot sun, sea urchins, gods, Roman inscriptions, white yacht-hulls. A man on the jetty is filling the blue sky with islands from his pipe.

Marakat's voice goes on, and in my mind's eye the brown figure of Death enters. It begins to shoot arrows at the men and women and at the musicians whose souls, suspended above them, are naked, like prawns.

I hear Marakat say, 'A rock-fall on the line behind the town. The Nice express is brought to a halt by it. The train is delayed long enough that some of the passengers spend the night at the hotel in which the accused is staying.'

So these are the last moments during which I am ignorant of Marakat's revelation, when things remain, for a few seconds, as they have always been before. In future there will always be life as it was before Mr. Marakat's revelation, and life after it. What is it that, for all this time, I have not known or been unable to remember?

Marakat pauses, then says, grinning, 'Among these passengers is a young black woman who is Ottoline Hodler.'

Throughout my life I have been hoping to see the passengers off the Menton train again. I have spent my time thinking I saw them where they did not exist, recognising strangers mistakenly, grasping at characters that belong in oblivion. I have stumbled about in no-man's land, a wanderer who has lost his powers of observation. I listen with horror as Marakat, with his leisurely sentences, transforms the high-spirited woman at Menton, my childhood Lipstick Matabele, into the patient and repressed Ottoline Hodler. I had forgotten that sadness can change people beyond recognition.

I feel torment and guilt, my brain is outlawed by itself. My life is misremembered, then cruelly re-arranged. Just when you have the answer, you turn out to be mistaken. Time, place and circumstance are the enemies of philosophy and music.

Marakat: 'I know for a fact that she and the accused became friends, *camarades*.'

Puisat: 'So quickly?'

Marakat: 'I saw them steal a motorbike and ride it to the Italian frontier. Afterwards they provoked a fight between hotel waiters during which one of the waiters was injured.'

Puisat: 'In what way injured?'

Marakat: 'Bitten.'

Puisat: 'So you would describe the accused and Ottoline Hodler as being immediately intimate.'

Marakat: 'I saw them go to her room. At dinner they talked earnestly together and held hands.'

Courbot, jumping up and forgetting for once the difference between being natural and being real: 'He was a child at the time.'

Puisat: 'Twelve.'

Courbot: 'A child, precisely. To him the young woman he met briefly when he was a child was unrecognizable as the same person when he met her again in Switzerland much later. He hardly noticed Ottoline Hodler. To him the two are, and always have been, separate women.'

Puisat: 'Separate women?'
Courbot: 'Separate women.'

<u>**29**</u>

On the evening after Mr. Marakat makes his revelation, when I come into my room I see at once that I am already seated at my table. The figure springs up and leaps at me. He lands on my back and, clinging like a monkey, wraps one long arm across my eyes.

Since then I have been able to write next to nothing. My letters to myself have lapsed, Spofforth goes away empty-handed, and in the meantime it has become winter.

I know this because the reinforced window of the prison van has daily become the frame for a little winter view of the river. The Seine is frozen and I can see that snow dumped from Pont St-Michel is heaped in conical piles on the ice. It is a cruel view. People are starving. A cart-horse, lying on its side on the Quai d'Orfèvres, is being whipped on the face by its driver to make it get up. A funeral bell is tolling at ten-second intervals, and the bereaved sky wears black and yellow-grey.

And each day, over and over, I think to myself something along these lines, as follows:

And not only you. I have been a long time with you in hell. I am grown out of myself into other existences. My mind is full of a teeming cast of strangers and I sleep with my eyes open. Don't you know who I am? And can't you tell where I am not?

Hello, Corruption. Hello, Loss. Have you nothing to say to me, Disappointment and Inevitability? Feel free to address me on the subject of vacancy. Oh, I have judged with judges, pranced with critics, ranted in pulpits, enjoyed little bursts of gaieté de coeur with lawyers and enormous eaters. One good horse's laugh with Beethoven is worth a year of aphorisms.

Listen, I don't give a damn about it anymore. None of it troubles me. Change places as often as you like and I will simply change writers. I and my childhood are strangers, one to another. There is something at the very centre of my being which can be taught absolutely nothing. I have lived with a murderer and never even suspected him. Did you divide me, me from me? Who made this false margin? Who forced me to sit here and watch the sea, the inept sea, wave-less, hazy, like an invalid between waking and sleeping? Whatever any of you says, no squirming, no metaphysics, can prevent the caterers' uncontrollable laughter or revise the forces of darkness which stopped me from being good.

You forget, *cher psychopath*, that I am inveterate when it comes to contradictions and confusions, the signs of life. You think the universe has given up humming?

I it was who saw the train hot and bothered when it was halted by the rock-fall. I who saw the monkey on the beach, the pediment split at Paestum, the doppelgänger in Oxford, the seven of clubs which killed my father, who died laughing. I it was who looked into the eyes of the eel, discovered the garden to be imaginary, was overwhelmed by silence in the mountains, watched the pulse of nature frozen, and failed disastrously to recognise Lipstick Matabele.

Such memories do not easily make for a parliament of apathy, I can tell you, not even absent-mindedly in Naples.

And now, do tell me before my name is adjusted yet again. Do tell me, without rancour, how is the Dutch ventriloquist?

For I had thought that this was just the beginning, but it turns out to be the end. For, being several, I had hoped to live. For I had thought to last forever, outlasting life itself, but find myself steadily dismantled, piece by piece, passion by passion, hope by hope, towards some thorough detachment of which I had not the slightest inkling. For I missed the trial. For I did not even read the book. For I slept between one sleep and another, died between one death and another, and now I am found out.

For had I understood the life sentence, I might have understood the trial.

I leave these fragments to be dug up, dwindled, faded, slowly worn out by time, amounting to very little, but at least dug up like Freud's tomb figures in the end and exhibited to the daylight as traces of a human being, and of expired convictions.

★

Puisat approaches the conclusion of his cross-examination in these terms. It comes to the penultimate week.

Puisat, to me: 'You are your own worst enemy. Your own worst enemy.'

Me: 'Isn't everybody?'

Puisat: 'That you are your own worst enemy is what, in effect, you have been pleading throughout this trial.'

Me: 'No. what I have pleaded is that I'm innocent of Ottoline Hodler's death.'

Puisat, hectoring: 'On the contrary. You have shown that, at the very least, you have been in two minds and afraid of your own shadow.'

Me: 'No. I have simply been true to myself.'

Puisat, changing tack, as he has done frequently for months: 'Ottoline Hodler knew your identity.'

Me: 'I did not know hers.'

Puisat: 'And, knowing that you draw sometimes, she went so far as to ask for your help. Not for herself. For, of all things, a charity she supported.'

Me: 'She never at any time asked me for anything.'

Puisat: 'I think she did. Does the name of it mean nothing to you?'

Me: 'I do not know its name.'

Puisat: 'Pencils for Matabeleland. She believed that all children should draw. It is certain that she asked you about it because there is a letter from you which refers to it.'

Me: 'I have told you that I never wrote to her.'

Puisat: 'How strange, when all these letters which were

found in her possession are undeniably in your handwriting.'
Me: 'She never asked me.'
Puisat: 'But a letter in your own writing?'
Me: 'Why should I have written to her when we lived in the same hotel?'
Puisat: 'You deny writing it?'
Me: 'Yes. I speak the truth, laughing.'
Puisat: 'What?'
Me: 'Horace. I was quoting Horace.'
Puisat: 'You could have saved her.'
Me: 'I could.'
Puisat: 'You could have saved her but chose not to.'
Me: 'I was almost unaware of her. Had it not been for the invalid I would hardly have noticed her.'
Puisat: 'You spoke to her, wrote to her several times.'
Me: 'I was in an anteroom of suggestion. Had my painting been interrupted I would have become someone else.'
Puisat: 'Become who?'
But I do not reply to his question. I am thinking of Lipstick Matabele, the only woman I have ever much liked. I suppose I loved her.
At last I say, 'Even to kill yourself is to reinvent your identity.'

And then the end comes very quickly. Puisat, in a whirl of gown, jumps to his feet and, ignoring the judges, shouts, 'Then who were you?'
Me: 'I did not exist at that point because I had no idea which of them was me.'
Puisat leans, looming, towards me and yells, 'Which of who? WHICH OF WHO?'
Which of who strikes me as his first reasonable question for weeks and, without acrimony, I turn it over in my mind. Which of who is after all at the heart of the matter before we all die. Do you not find sometimes that what you know is what you do not know, that what you do not know is the only truth that has entered your head with any certainty?

It is now that in another man's voice I begin to sing. We shared the same views and turns of speech to such an extent that talking to him was like talking to myself. The court keeps silent while I sing these words which I never learned and do not know.

> My doubles, unidentified,
> None the less are me.
> Misdated,
> Misattributed,
> Hidden kin are we.
>
> Jointed to the hollow tide,
> Bending hollow knee,
> Maddened lobster,
> Boiling mind
> But none the less me.
>
> Cortège of shadows,
> Genealogy.
> Every human being
> A penal colony.
>
> I invented Egypt.
> I reinvented me.
> Misremembered, misremembering
> Auto
> Biography.
>
> Dark the delusions
> Of psychiatry.
> Far darker the
> Delusions which
> Reason keeps from me.
>
> Still I am the other
> If alter egos be,

Paranoid,
Delirious,
But none the less free.

★

From your perch in the future, reader, you probably know what happened next. I do not. It is in the nature of autobiography that the author does not know his end or subsequent reputation, whereas the reader may. As for you, *cher psychopath,* you also are left guessing. Having revised your identity and mine so often, I will not presume to write a further word about them. Have I known the dimensions of your life but missed the poetry of it? Measured you while you were still alive, without peeling back the blankets, and ended up writing a square coffin? Probably by now both measurer and measured are no longer living, the songbird and the listener both dead, the song and the enchanted ear both extinct. The only paradise we shall know is a fool's paradise.

So now, while temporarily in your right mind, sign our name, reader. Do it while you feel as sane as the next person, and in the process answer a cloud of questions about the randomness of life and a whole library of the unknown. Do it quickly, before being interrupted by the drunk who approaches, shouting and blowing a whistle. Here, I will write it out for you in the innocent form of a letter's ending:

I beg you to accept, dear Second Self, our sincere compliments.
Je vous prie d'accepter mes très sincères salutations.
Bien amicalement.

....
(Signed by you, the reader, and duly dated.)

P.S. There remains the judgment. Next week when they drag one or all of me into court for the last time, I shall say to you and to the judges as follows:

'Condemn me, but tell me who I am **FIRST**.'